MW00878687

Stolen

Innocence

"A Tainted Love Affair"

By Betty Knight Taylor

This book is not to be duplicated or copied by anyone other than the author.

The characters in this story does not pertain to anyone or their life this is fiction romance mystery.

© copyright 2012 Betty Knight Taylor

Introduction

Vanessa carter is a beautiful intelligent young woman, graduating top of her high school class with a bright future ahead of her. Vanessa is popular and loved by her class mates, comes from a respected home, inexperienced to the ways of the world, Vanessa's life takes a dramatic turn at her class graduation party. Vanessa finds her world has been turned upside down after a gruesome discovery nevertheless, the puzzle has pieces missing. Frantic, heartbroken and confused, until her longtime friend Jarvis offers to help her through a turbulent time. Will Jarvis be the man of her dreams? Or will he be the nightmare see can't seem to awaken from?

Friday Night Graduation Party

Music, Lights and alcohol makes for a wild night for teens especially an unsupervised affair. Trouble looms in the air when a young girl life is changed forever. The fight for her life begins in ways she will never imagine.

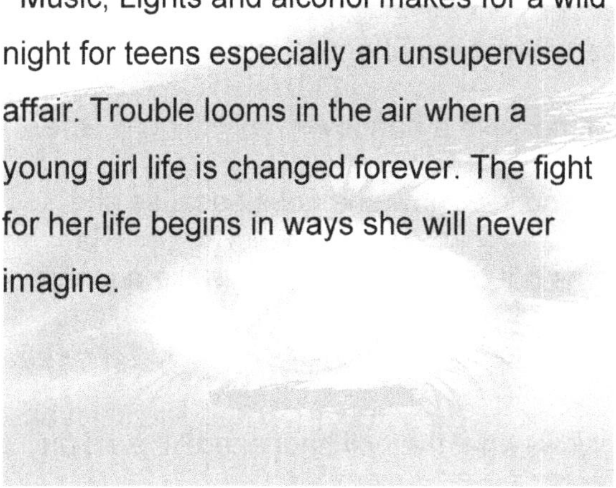

The next morning

The birds are singing outside of Vanessa's window, it's a bright sunny Saturday morning in June. The graduation party Vanessa attended last evening has left her with a hangover, only thing is, she has no idea how she got it because she does not drink. Vanessa feels like a ton of dry concrete is sitting on her head.

"Wow, what the hell happened? How did I get here?"

Vanessa whispering as she is slowly getting out of bed.

"Vanessa, Tiffany come to breakfast" hollers their mom Kathleen from downstairs. Tiffany just walks into Vanessa's room looking Vanessa up and down.

"What do you want you lil brat get out of my room" screams Vanessa.

"Well, well, well, are you sure you want me to leave with all this information I have for mom & dad" asked Tiffany.

"What are you talking about" ask Vanessa as she is barely making it. "Well, now my dear sister you are going to have to bargain for this juicy info" says Tiffy. "What you want?" asks Vanessa as she is looking hard at Tiffy. "Let's start with your ipod and that baby blue tank top" "are you kidding me Tiffy?" "uh, no" " Forget about it Tiffy no top or ipod beat it get out of my room before I dump you on your head" Tiffany looks at Vanessa and says "ok I guess Mom & Dad will be interested in knowing how you got home last night from Sheka's graduation party!" Vanessa hurries and closes her bedroom door. "What did you see?"

"No deal no info"

Vanessa rethinks Tiffy's deal

"Ok, ok here take it, now tell me what happened because it is all a big blur"

"Well Sheka called me on my cell and told me to open the door and not to wake anybody so I opened the door and there you were drunk as a skunk they had to literally pick you up and bring you upstairs and lay you in the bed I took your shoes off and covered you up, what happened over there?"

"Tiffy not a word of this please cause I don't know what happened, all I remember is drinking some punch and now I am home and I am sick as a dog"

"Girls get your butts down to breakfast right now" screams Terry the girls' father. "Tiffy tell Mom I have cramps and can't make it

ok"

"Ok, I guess I better get down there, Tiffy looks back as she is about to leave and says "Vanessa you should pick better friends it's something about Sheka that urks me" Tiffy goes downstairs and kisses her dad

"Hey princess where's Vanessa?" ask Terry

"Oh, Mom Vanessa is cramping and can't come down"

"I better go check on my baby after breakfast" says Kathleen.

Vanessa stumbles to the bathroom and throws up, then notices that her panties are soaking wet.

"What the hell is this, oh my God I know I didn't have sex, I couldn't have, or did I, what happened?"

Vanessa is frantic and runs to get her cell phone and calls Sheka but get no answer, Vanessa leaves a voice mail

"Sheka girl call me as soon as you get this message I am tripping I need to know what happened last night." Just then Kathleen knocks at the door.

“Hey sweetie it’s me Mom, I brought you a hot cup of peppermint tea to help your cramps.”

“Come in Mom”

“Awe, you look beat up here drink this it will make you feel better ok, get some rest and I will check on you later.”

“Thanks Mom” Vanessa drinks the tea the warmth is helping her stomach to settle but her head is still pounding. Vanessa can’t help but wonder what happened it is all a mystery to her and it is driving her to tears. Sheka returns Vanessa’s call

“Hey Nessa girl what’s up?”

"Sheka girl I am tripping how did I get drunk?"

"I guess from all that punch you had somebody must have spiked it."

"That's messed up, if I would have known that I would not have drank any of that shit."

"Calm down Nessa, it was a party and we graduated from High school most of us like yourself will be leaving for college soon so just suck it up and forget about it."

"I can't Sheka, did I do something stupid?"

"Naw girl you was cool you were just having fun then you passed out and we brought you home."

"Who's we Sheka?"

"Me and Jarvis, my boyfriend, remember."

"Oh, ok I guess I should just leave it alone but, no more drinking punch for me that's the first and last time I will feel like this."

"So you want to go to the mall later Nessa, I need to pick up some things before heading off to Atlanta, it's going to be a big relief to get away from dry ass Florida, so what you say want to go?"

"Not this trip I pass I feel like something ran me over."

"Ok well, I got to get going I will talk to you later hope you feel better call me." "Yea, later"

The girls hang up and Vanessa goes to the bathroom to get some Advil for her huge headache.

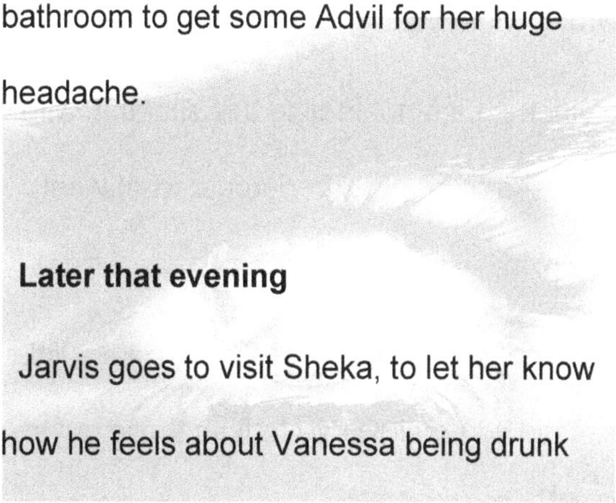

Later that evening

Jarvis goes to visit Sheka, to let her know how he feels about Vanessa being drunk last night.

"Hey Jarvis baby what's up? Come in and have a seat I will be right back I need to wash my hands." Sheka goes to wash her hands and Jarvis have a seat in the living room.

As sheka is walking into the living room she is looking at Jarvis sideways. “What’s wrong with you J?”

“Sheka, I am not feeling this situation with Vanessa man, I feel bad about what went down.”

“It’s not our fault she was acting like a little slut did you really have to fight those guys looks to me like you were defending her what’s the deal Jarvis?”

“That’s not what happened Sheka, I thought she was your friend.”

"It was your friends J not mine."

"Yea but I didn't think Odell and his friends would mess with her."

Odell was older, already in his second year of college in Texas. He was visiting for the summer with some of his college friends and wanted to party and found the perfect opportunity with Vanessa knocked out cold on Sheka's bed.

"I spoke with Vanessa earlier and she is cool she just have a bad hangover she will be ok just leave it alone, don't dare tell her what happened we don't need her freaking out you know how she is."

"But Sheka it was wrong don't you understand they RAPED HER!"

"Stop tripping J! Screams Sheka "the less she knows the better so you better keep your mouth shut!"

Jarvis walks out angry with Sheka as she is calling him back Jarvis just keeps walking and get into his car and leave. Sheka slams the door and calls Jarvis a bastard.

Back at Vanessa's she seems to feel a little better and goes downstairs with the rest of the family to watch movies.

"There's my graduate, says Terry, we are so proud of you and will be even prouder when you graduate from the best school in Texas!"

"So how was the party last night at Sheka's?" ask Kathleen.

"Oh it was ok I came home early so I could get some rest." Tiffy looking funny as though she is about to spill the big secret. Vanessa gets up to go in the kitchen to get a snack and notice that she has a bruise on her arm and leg. "Where did that come from? Now I am really confused, did I fall or what?" Vanessa quickly goes upstairs to get her robe so her parents do not see her bruises. Vanessa was about to head back downstairs and decided to go back to her room and watch movies alone.

The next morning

"Vanessa Hurry up we are late for church Calls Kathleen,

"Just a minute mom I will be right down" Vanessa is still reeling from Friday night, but decides to clear her mind church seems to be just the medicine she needs.

"Well, look at you, you are so beautiful Vanessa all the guys are going to start asking you out but they have to come through me first" Laughs Terry. Vanessa is a beautiful slender, caramel colored young woman with long flowing hair and a smile that is warm as the summer sun.

"Ok girls, you can sit with your friends but remember to listen to the word and meet your dad and me at the front of the church ok love you."

"Love you too mom" as Tiffany sees her friends. Vanessa see Sheka and Jarvis and go to see where they want to sit but Sheka see her and grab Jarvis and get lost in the crowd to avoid Vanessa.

"Why did you duck out from your girl" ask Jarvis.

“I don’t want to see her especially, when she starts whining about Friday night.”

“Sheka you are really beginning to surprise me, I never thought you would diss Vanessa this way.”

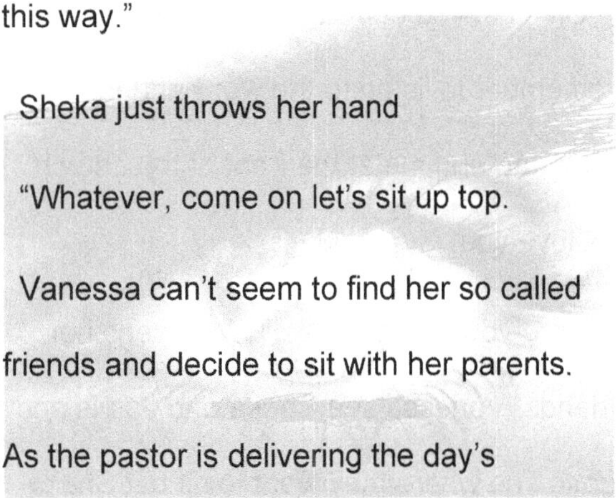

Sheka just throws her hand

“Whatever, come on let’s sit up top.

Vanessa can’t seem to find her so called friends and decide to sit with her parents. As the pastor is delivering the day’s message Vanessa mind keeps drifting back to the party, for some odd reason she can’t seem to shake it, just seem as so much more happened then Sheka is telling her.

Vanessa is not hearing a word the pastor is speaking for the racing thoughts that are captivating her mind. Church service is over and the ride home is silent. Everyone come in and go to get in comfortable clothing before dinner. Sunday dinner is always a big feast at the Carter's Kathleen has prepared Roast, potatoes, greens, cornbread, yams and peach cobbler for dessert one of Vanessa's favorite meals although, today Vanessa is just barely eating.

"What's wrong Vanessa you are hardly touching your plate I thought this is your favorite I cooked it just for you."

"I'm sorry Mom I just don't have much of an appetite right now may I be excused?"

Vanessa gets up and leaves the table her mom and dad look at one another with a puzzled look.

"Seems like Vanessa would be more excited about graduating and leaving for college in a month what you think the problem may be honey?" ask Kathleen to Terry

"I'm not sure, maybe it's the leaving home that has her in a dump she will be fine."

Tiffany just looks and has a question of concern in her mind as well.

"Thanks mom for the lovely dinner, I can clean the dishes I know its Vanessa turn but I can do it"

"Thanks baby that's sweet of you in the meantime I think I will talk to Vanessa." Kathleen goes up stairs to speak with Vanessa and find her crying.

"What's wrong sweetie?'

"Oh, nothing mom I am just a little teary about leaving home I am really going to miss you guys."

Of course Vanessa is lying, she is really upset about being drunk, not remembering and most of all she had semen in her panties and feels as though Sheka knows something she is not telling her.

“Oh, sweetheart it’s ok I remember when I left home for school, it was so scary I got sick but, once I got there and got settled in and started getting in the groove of things I loosened up and so will you ok.”

“Thanks Mom you always know how to make me feel better.”

Vanessa and her mom give each other a big hug.

“Now try and get some rest and I will talk to you later ok love you Vanessa” "love you too Mom" after Vanessa Mom leave the room Vanessa calls Sheka by now she is ready to demand that Sheka tell her what happened and she didn't want no jive about it. Vanessa get Sheka voicemail again.

"Sheka, listen you need to call me right away because for some reason I feel you are holding back on me about Friday night and you need to come straight with me, so call me when you get this message."

Vanessa feels like taking a drive so she gets her keys and head for the mall.

"Hey Daddy I am going to go to the mall for a little while."

"Ok baby are you ok do you need some money?"

"No, I'm cool, I still have the graduation gifts and most of them were money so I'm good thanks Daddy."

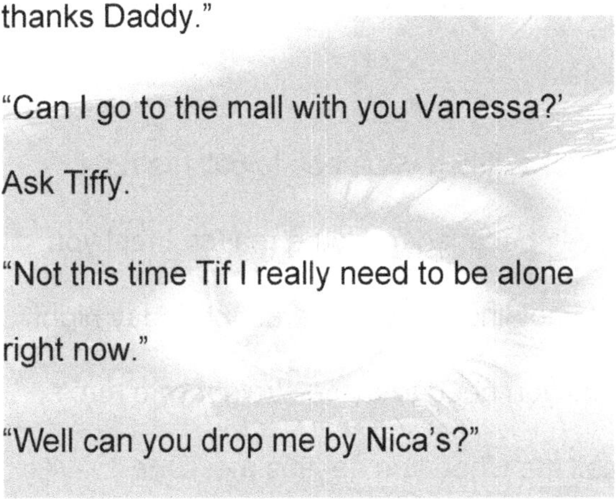

"Can I go to the mall with you Vanessa?' Ask Tiffy.

"Not this time Tif I really need to be alone right now."

"Well can you drop me by Nica's?"

"Make sure it's ok with Mom and Dad."

"It's ok just make sure you don't get into anything and be there when Vanessa come back for you."

"I will Daddy" as Tiffy runs out to the car.

"Ok here you are Tif I wonder if Draya is home."

Draya is Nica older sister and usually she will chat with Vanessa for a minute, they are not great friends but they talk from time to time. After Tiff goes in Vanessa notice Draya and two of her friends walking out.

"Hey Draya what's up girl?"

But Draya and her friend's just walk pass Vanessa pointing and laughing at her.

"What the hell was that all about? Something is fishy."

Vanessa just drives away now she is really concerned after seeing Draya. Vanessa parks and walk into the mall, as she is walking to her favorite store Macy's she see some more of her classmates that were at the party and they just look at her and one of the girls blurt out "SLUT" as they were walking fast away from Vanessa.

"Oh, hell naw, no that Bitch didn't look at me and say that!" you see because Vanessa is very popular and plus she is a virgin still at least that's what she thinks.

"Now it's really time to get to the bottom of this!"

Vanessa calls Jarvis

"Hello" answers Jarvis

"Hey what's up it's me Vanessa."

"Hey Vanessa what's going on with you girl?"

"Just in the mall listen, Jarvis I know you and Sheka brought me home Friday after the party I have no idea what happened. Can you clear up some things for me because everything is a big blur.

"What you mean Nessa?"

"Well, seems like something happened and everyone knows but me."

"Nothing happened out of the ordinary you just had some punch and passed out then we took you home that's all."

"You sure Jarvis, you not holding out on me are you?"

"No way girl, but look here I got to go so I will holler at you later ok."

Jarvis hangs up from nervousness. The real deal is when the party was about to wind down with just a few people remaining Odell and his friends showed up Jarvis was glad to see him because it's been years since Odell been to Florida, he and his Mother left when Odell was six and vowed never to return but Odell wanted to see family so he came for the summer break he is a student in his second year at Texas State. Any way Sheka added a little something to Vanessa punch that's why she passed out on the sofa.

Jarvis and sheka took her to Sheka's room to sleep it off. Odell and his friends wandering around went in the room and saw Vanessa passed out and decided to have some fun. Odell added a little date rape drug which made Vanessa a lot groggier when full sedated Odell's friends had their way with Vanessa. Jarvis got suspicious and found one of Odell's friends on Vanessa, that's when the fight ensued.

After they actually raped Vanessa Jarvis asked them to leave Odell was bragging how they did Vanessa as they were leaving.

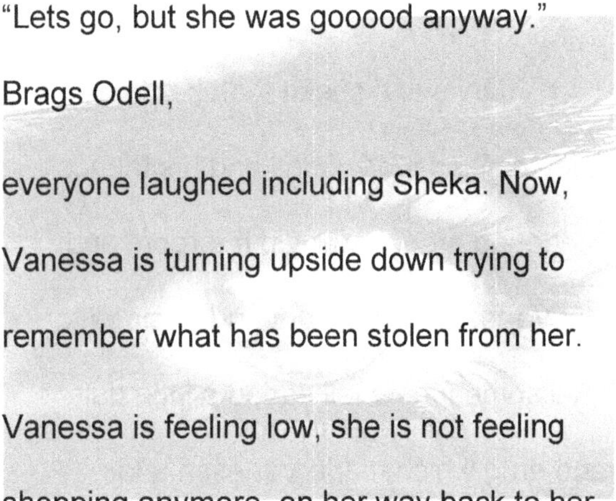

“Lets go, but she was gooood anyway.” Brags Odell,

everyone laughed including Sheka. Now, Vanessa is turning upside down trying to remember what has been stolen from her.

Vanessa is feeling low, she is not feeling shopping anymore, on her way back to her car she notice someone has left a note on her car.

"What's this?" Vanessa opens the note and to her horror someone has written "You need to be ashamed of yourself when you drink you should FUCK at a hotel SLUT."

Vanessa tears the note up and drive home crying and cussing she is feeling so embarrassed that someone thinks she is a slut. When Vanessa returns from picking up Tiff she walks in to find they have company.

"Oh hey Vanessa, look who's here you may not remember him because you were so young when they left, this is your first cousin Odell."

When Odell saw Vanessa he was about to throw up he looked as though someone stuck a needle in him and drained all his blood. Vanessa extends her hands with no idea that Odell was at the party.

"Hello, it's nice to meet you."

Odell could barely shake Vanessa's hand without feeling like he was going to pass out.

"It's nice to meet you as well, say uncle Terry I really got to get going I am leaving early in the morning, just thought I would stop by and say hello and wish you and Mom would mend your differences it really will help the family and it was nice to meet you cuz."

"Well, you know Odell your Mom has been very stubborn I have tried calling her several times over the years but you are right and seeing you has changed me forever I love you nephew, I wish you would stay longer and get to know Vanessa & Tiff, you know Vanessa is leaving for College in a month or so".

"I can't I promised Mom I would be back so we could spend some time together this summer, but, good luck Vanessa I wish you well."

Odell quickly walks to his car he is terrified and now shame at how he allowed his stupidness to get him caught up. Odell arrives at Jarvis house without calling. “Hey what you want man?”

“I didn’t know that girl Vanessa is my cousin.” Jarvis is stunned

“What!”

Odell is tore up holding his head

“Man, dam I fucked up on this one, but it seems like she don’t know cause she didn’t remember me, ah, man how could I be so stupid I started to go over there Thursday man I wish I would have went over then I would have known dam!” “Look Odell man that was foul what your friends did Vanessa didn't deserve that. You need to leave just get out of town so no one finds out."

"You right I need to get out of here so I can get on the road I was going to stay but I better head out and just forget about this shit man."

"Yea dude, you need to leave."

"Jarvis I do feel bad though but this secret I need you to keep please don't tell this to nobody man."

"Nothing will come from me unless someone else knows that I can't guarantee."

"Alright Jarvis man I'm out."

Jarvis walks back into the house and calls sheka.

"Sheka, listen, Vanessa called me and wanted to know about Friday night." "What did you tell her?"

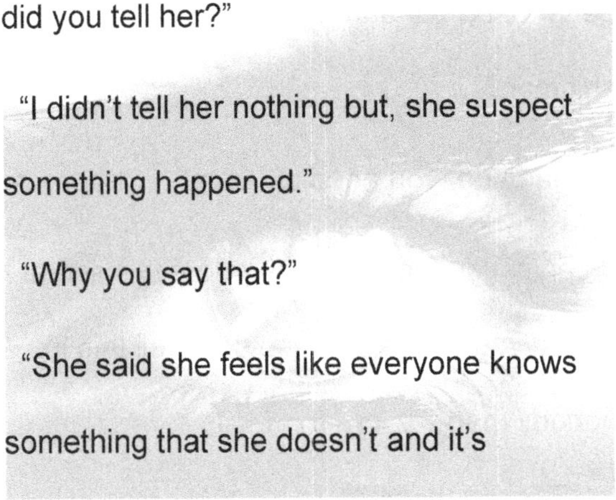

"I didn't tell her nothing but, she suspect something happened."

"Why you say that?"

"She said she feels like everyone knows something that she doesn't and it's beginning to trip me out, what if she got pregnant or something?"

"Why you worried, if she did so what, so stop sweating about it Jarvis, dam." "You suppose to be her friend; I think you should tell her something, anything and get this cleared up just in case that did happen."

"No way and far as her being my friend, think again I was just playing her cause she used to be popular but not anymore."

"I can't believe you Sheka, I thought you were better than that."

"Oh no you didn't say that to me you better check yourself Jarvis and if you say anything I will say you did it and I didn't know anything."

"Oh really well guess what I'm not going to say anything but far as you and me we're through!" Jarvis hangs up, Sheka frantically calls him back but Jarvis does not answer her call. Back at Vanessa's she is in her room trying to sort out things when she calls one of her other friends Tammy.

"Hey Tammy its Vanessa"

"Yea what's going on Vanessa?"

"Listen was you at the party when I passed out?"

"Well…. Yea"

"Please Tammy tell me what happened, everybody seem to know something I don't so can you clear this big blur up for me?"

"There is nothing to clear up you danced then went to sleep when everybody was leaving Jarvis and Sheka took you home." Tammy is lying because everyone there was sworn to secrecy by Sheka cause she knows how to bully others the handful of people that was there is keeping there mouths shut.

"Ok girl, it just seems crazy but I trust you would tell me if I made a fool of myself."

"So Vanessa are you ready for school I heard some people are getting in early for classes before the semester starts if they want to."

"Yea, I received a letter for early admission and I will be leaving the end of next month."

"Cool, I hope I get a letter because I need to get away right now. Well, I got to go help my Mother I will talk to you later Vanessa."

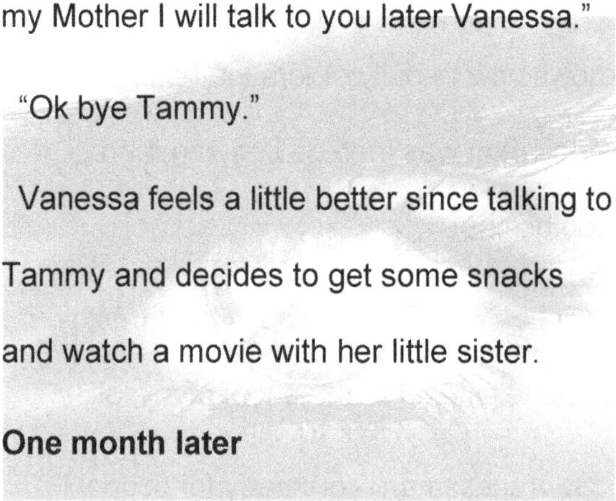

"Ok bye Tammy."

Vanessa feels a little better since talking to Tammy and decides to get some snacks and watch a movie with her little sister.

One month later

Vanessa is excited about leaving in three days for school, seems like she was just in fifth grade yesterday now she is leaving for Texas in three days.

"Hey my college bound child" Kathleen hugs Vanessa, how are you this morning? Listen, how would you like to go shopping with me so I can buy you some of those crazy clothes you youngsters wearing these days?"

"Well, somebody is in a good mood this morning, however, I will take you up on your offer mom, it will be my pleasure to shop with you and max out daddy's credit cards."

But in the back of Vanessa's mind she is worried that her period is late. Trying not to think about the night of the party Vanessa shakes her head and goes upstairs to get ready for her shopping trip. Although, she is excited about going shopping and leaving for school Vanessa find herself with a deep sadness that has suddenly overcome her and goes into her bathroom and cry intensely in the shower.

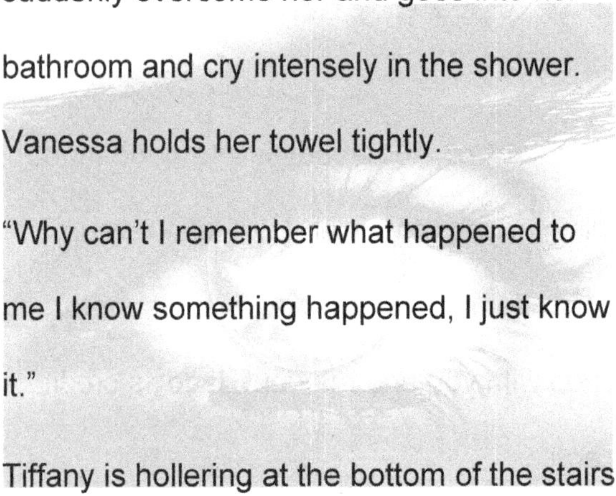

Vanessa holds her towel tightly.

"Why can't I remember what happened to me I know something happened, I just know it."

Tiffany is hollering at the bottom of the stairs "VANESSA, MAMA SAID HURRY UP WE ARE ABOUT TO LEAVE YOU." Vanessa running down the stairs

"Ok brat you don't have to holler like you in the woods."

Kathleen is handling her Mercedes Benz 500 and turns the radio up a notch

"Oh, this is my song" as Kathleen is singing along the girls is laughing at her. "What, I can sing honey."

"Sure you can mom" as Vanessa is looking at Tiffany and they both laugh again. The three ladies are having the time of their lives as they enter the mall Vanessa see Sheka and two other girls.

"Hey sheka girl where have you been I called you a couple of times what's up?"

"Oh, nothing much just been busy trying to get everything together for school you know"

"Yeah, I know, wow three more days and we will be leaving for school aren't you excited sheka?"

"Yes mam, hey you want to get together later and catch a movie or something?"

"Sure, I'll call you when me and Mom is finished."

"Ok I'll see you later." They depart and Vanessa is smiling.

"So what's going on with you?" ask Kathleen,

"Oh Sheka and I made a movie date for this evening, unless, you have something for me to do."

"No sweetheart, go have a good time after all it will be a while before you see your friends again."

"Hey can I come?" ask Tiffy

"Well, ok Tiffy seeing that I am leaving soon and won't see your little bratty face for a while."

Tiffy smiles at Vanessa with excitement, thinking how cool it will be to hang out with her big sister before she leaves.

Back at the house

"Hey daddy, we're home" hollers Tiffy

"Hey beautiful ladies I see ya'll been spending all my hard earned money."

"Yes, my husband we certainly have can you get the other bags out the car please?"

"Other bags what did you buy the whole store?"

"No but if you want dinner tonight you might want to get those bags."

Vanessa says hello to her father and go upstairs to get ready for the movies.

Vanessa's phone rings and its Jarvis

"Hey Vanessa, what's up I wanted to say hello before you leave for school." "That's sweet of you."

"So what you got planned before you leave?"

"Well, Sheka and I are going to the movies tonight, tomorrow I am going to dinner with my parents and then I think I will be finishing up on packing so I can get to school, so what are you doing before you leave?"

"About the same, I am ready to go so I can get started on my career."

"I bet you are excited about going to school with Sheka huh?"

"Well… Vanessa, Sheka and me broke up."

"Why?"

"I just think it would be better for the both of us if we gave each other same space."

"But you guys had so many plans."

"I know but that's all changed now, and if you don't mind I rather not talk about it ok."

"Ok cool, listen J I need to run so I will talk to you before I go."

"Ok Nessa and if I don't hear from you or see you I wish you the best in everything you are doing."

"Thanks J same to you bye."

When they hang up the phone Jarvis feels a little relief after talking to Vanessa. Tiffy knocks at Vanessa door.

"Hey can I come in?"

"Sure brat what do I owe the pleasure?"

"I just want to say thanks for letting me hang out with you tonight and to tell you that I love you and will miss you when you leave."

"Wow Tif I love you too brat and we are going to have a good time tonight so go get ready we are leaving in about 10 minutes ok." Tiffany smiles and leaves. Vanessa calls Sheka to make sure they are still on but Sheka does not answer Vanessa leaves a message for her to call back. After 30 minutes Sheka still is not answering her phone so Vanessa decides to go to the movies anyway with Tiffany.

"So Vanessa is we still meeting up with your gross friend Sheka?"

"She is not gross and I am not sure, she didn't answer when I called her. I hope she is waiting on us at the movies."

"I hope not she is gross and I don't like her Vanessa."

"Why don't you like Sheka?"

"She just seems so fake."

Vanessa just looks at Tiffy as they are getting out of the car.

"I don't see Sheka, I hope nothing has happened to her."

"I don't think she is coming so let's just go in and forget about her."

"Let's just wait a few minutes we still have time before the movie starts and if she is not here in 10 minutes we will go in ok." 10 minutes have passed and still no Sheka so Vanessa and Tiffany go into the theater.

"Man, Vanessa that was a good movie, can we get some ice cream before we go home?"

"Sure, I wonder what happened to Sheka."

"Forget about that hood rat she just playing you Vanessa, I keep telling you she's not your friend, friends don't trip like that."

"You seem to know too much for a little thirteen year old."

"That's because I'm smart." Tiffany licks her ice cream with a smile.

"Tiffany, you're ok for a brat." Vanessa smiles at Tiffy.

"Come on brat let's get home so we can start our day again tomorrow, we have a dinner date with mom and dad.

Vanessa is taking a shower and suddenly feels sick to her stomach.

"I need to lay down, man, my stomach is so creasy I must have ate too much." Before Vanessa goes to bed she tries Sheka again, still no answer. Sheka has seen every call from Vanessa and has ignored everyone.

"I wish she would stop calling me. What a loser."

Sheka keeps partying with her other so called friends. Vanessa decides to call it a night.

The next morning Vanessa is still feeling nauseated but decides to get up and move around in hopes of feeling better so she can get to activities with the family. Vanessa goes down stairs and the family is waiting at the table Kathleen has cooked Bacon, eggs, toast, hash browns and grits.

"What's all this?" ask Vanessa

"I thought I would cook your favorite breakfast before you leave tomorrow, oh Vanessa I am going to miss you so much." Kathleen begins to tear.

"Oh mom I am going to miss you all too, don't cry I will see you soon and I promise to make you real proud of me."

"That's my girl." Adds Terry

Vanessa is trying to eat without letting anyone know she is feeling sick, she don't want to ruin the family day especially when her mom has went to so much trouble with cooking.

"May I be excused I need to go get dressed for our day."

"But you have hardly touched your food honey are you ok?" Kathleen is concerned.

"Oh I am fine I just need to get dressed I'm excited."

Vanessa runs upstairs and once in her room she is in the bathroom vomiting.

"What is wrong with me?"

Vanessa is beginning to get worried and goes back to the night she got drunk.

"Something had to happen and I need to know what but everybody keep telling me nothing happened. What am I going to do?"

Kathleen is knocking at the door

"Vanessa, are you ok?"

"Yea mom I will be down in a minute."

"Ok, we will be leaving for the museum in about thirty minutes."

"Right, I will be ready mom."

Vanessa is frantic, feeling sick and confused she dresses in a beautiful pink outfit with the shoes to match and makes her face and hair. Vanessa is looking beautiful as she strolls down stairs and leaves with her family.

"It is a beautiful day" Vanessa breathes in the summer air.

"Yes it is." Comments Tiffy.

The family has had a big day with the museum, a fashion show and topped with an expensive dinner to wish Vanessa success at school.

Everyone is tired and ready for bed because Vanessa will fly out early. "Thanks everybody today was so good, but I better get some sleep so I can be ready to leave in the morning."

"Ok sweetheart get some rest we will see you in the morning, love you good night." As Terry hugs Vanessa.

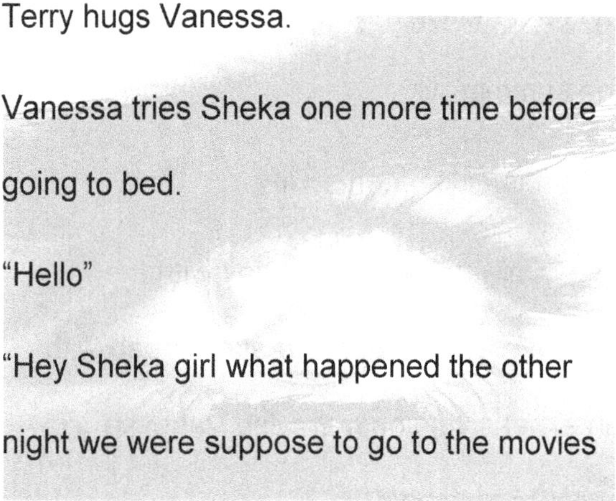

Vanessa tries Sheka one more time before going to bed.

"Hello"

"Hey Sheka girl what happened the other night we were suppose to go to the movies where were you?"

"Oh, I got tied up my bad, I guess we will have to do something another time."

"It won't be soon I'm leaving early in the morning for Texas."

"Is it that time already, well, maybe on break we can get together how about that?"

"Ok, I will keep in touch, when are you leaving?"

"In about two weeks."

"Oh yea Sheka what happened with you and J he told me you guys broke up."

"Really, that's strange I don't recall us breaking up he just left here and we were cool."

Of course Sheka is lying she's been begging Jarvis since he broke it off.

"Oh, well, you know how men are I guess he was just tripping I know you are happy about him going to school with you."

"Yes I am and we are getting married when we get settled."

"That's great, but are you sure you want to do that before getting your education Sheka?"

"Well, it won't be right away we are going to wait until our senior year. Listen, Vanessa I got to go I wish you a safe trip and I will talk to you soon girl."

"Thanks Sheka I will talk to you soon bye."

Sheka is furious when she hangs up.

"That Bastard Jarvis told this Bitch my business well fuck him I don't need him."

But Sheka is really hurt and cries.

The next morning Vanessa, college bound

Vanessa is up and ready to go, but still feeling sick.

"This is crazy I need to get a hold of myself, I know it's just my nerves because I am leaving home. That's it I'm just tripping."

Vanessa trying to reassure herself it's all in her mind.

"Well, you ready?" Terry stands strong as he opens the car door for his favorite girls.

"Now remember Vanessa, to call us as soon as you get into your dorm, also don't forget to be polite and work hard."

"Mom relax I won't forget."

They finally reach the airport, everyone is saying their goodbyes. Tiffany hugs Vanessa tight, Kathleen is crying, Terry is smiling proudly.

"Oh, I almost forgot Vanessa, here's your credit card. Please be responsible your limit is Two Thousand dollars a month so try to stay within the limit ok."

Terry is looking at Vanessa with great hopes.

"I got ya Daddy; I think I can manage that." Vanessa waves as she walks toward her gate. Once on the plane Vanessa cries and starts to feel sick again.

"May I have some Ginger ale?"

"Sure can."

The stewardess gets Vanessa a cold cup of Ginger ale.

Vanessa has finally landed in the great state of Texas. Vanessa grabs her bags and head for the campus. Upon her arrival she is greeted by a team of administration and led to the orientation to find out the campus rules and where her dorm is.

"Hello everyone, I am Mrs. Duncan one of the counselors here. I want to welcome you all, this orientation takes about two hours with a 15 minute break in that time you will have the tools to get started with your first semester of school." Finally a break, Vanessa is nervous.

"Hello, my name is Tranetta, I saw you over here alone and decided to join you I hope I'm not bothering you."

"Oh no I'm Vanessa nice to meet you."

Tranetta is nervous as well, Tranetta is a tall Almond colored young woman with dark overtones, sassy dresser, kind of stuck up with sprinkles of ghetto.

"Vanessa girl I am so nervous I have never been this far from home alone."

"So where are you from?" ask Vanessa.

"I'm from Atlanta, where are you from Vanessa?"

"I'm from a small town in Florida."

"Looks like it's time to head back in, so would you like to sit together Vanessa?"

"Sure why not."

Orientation is over the groups split into four each and is guided to their dorms.

"Ok Vanessa, I guess I'll see you around."

Tranetta is looking a little sad.

"Yea, maybe we can have lunch."

The girls go to their groups. Vanessa is excited as the dorm Manager unlocks her dorm door. The place is fabulous with a living room area, small quaint kitchen area, and two small bedrooms and a bath. The dorm manager Felicia gives Vanessa the keys and tells her that her room mate should be coming soon.

"Thanks, for your help Ms. Felicia."

"No problem Vanessa if you need anything just let me know I am in hall c ok." Just then who walks in; Tranetta.

"Well, well, well, who would have thought, but, secretly Vanessa I was hoping I would get you as my room mate."

"This is great."

Tranetta and Vanessa hit it off right away.

"So Vanessa have you picked your room yet?"

"As a matter of fact I have, I took the room that faces the court yard those beautiful flowers attracted me."

“Cool, but look at this view from my room you can see the city, wow look at that.”

“This is beautiful, but I still love my view.”

“So it’s settled you like you room and I like mine I think we are off to a good start.”

“Yes, we are, oh I almost forgot I need to call my parents and let them know how I’m doing.”

“Cool I’m going to go unpack and shower.”

Vanessa goes to her room to call her parents.

“Hello Mom, I am all in, the campus is beautiful and my dorm is great, I also have a pretty cool room mate.”

"That's great Vanessa, I know you are excited but try not to be too friendly until you get to know her better what's her name?"

"Her name is Tranetta Ferguson and she is from Atlanta, very pretty girl."

"Oh, she's from the big city, well you're not so be cool young lady."

"Oh mom you worry too much, where's dad and Tif?"

"They went to the store I will make sure to tell them you called and we will call you after dinner tonight ok, love you baby miss you already."

“Love and miss you too mom talk to you later.”

Vanessa is in the kitchen looking around when Tranetta walks in.

“Cute place huh?”

“Yea I was just looking around and admiring how cool this place is, I thought it would be bland and boring but I guess I got a great surprise.”

“Me too, so did you call home?”

“Yes I did and everyone is good. Now, it’s my time to shower, and after that go get some food in this place.”

"I was thinking the same thing there is actually a supermarket on campus how cool is that?'

"That is cool, I will only be a few minutes then we can go get some things we need."

"For sure but take your time Vanessa, I will be in the living room."

After twenty minutes Vanessa walks out in a gorgeous Dereon outfit with the purse and shoes to match.

"Look at you girl that outfit is hot." Tranetta is looking pretty fly herself in Baby Phat.

"So do you Tranetta, I love baby Phat as well, are you ready to go?"

"Yes mam after you."

They girls walk to the super market and discover many fascinating places as they stroll around.

"Vanessa, look is that a shopping mall?"

"Oh my God it is I know where I'm going tomorrow for sure." They both giggle as they continue on to the super market.

"This place is huge." Vanessa is excited. The girls each get a shopping cart and get the things they need. Vanessa is thinking how blessed she is to have the opportunity to come to a prestigious university and have parents who support her. "I have to remember to shop wisely I am limited so I must stick to the basics." Once again the nausea starts just when Vanessa smells the bread baking in the bakery. "Ok enough of this I know I'm not pregnant but just to be sure I am going to get a test." Vanessa walks over to the pharmacy on the way she see Tranetta in an aisle and wave to her. "Hey Vanessa I will meet you at check out in about ten minutes is that good?" "Sure I'll be ready see you there." Vanessa is beginning to really feel nauseated and quickly looks over the pregnancy test to see which one is best. "This is crazy." Vanessa whispers to herself as she picks the clear blue with the easy instructions.

"Hey we timed this right meeting at the check out line together. I didn't get much I have to wait on some money coming this week."

"Oh it's cool Tranetta I have plenty how about I cook tonight?"

Vanessa has hid the pregnancy test under other items in her cart and trying to figure out how she is going to get it paid for without Tranetta finding out her business.

Tranetta puts her things on the belt when Vanessa notices a lane open 2 lanes away.

"There is another lane open I think I will go over there this way it will be quick for us both."

"Ok cool meet you at the door."

"Ok" Vanessa is thinking "Boy that was close." Vanessa pays for her items and puts the test in her purse.

"Alright Ms. Tranetta lets head back to our spot." The ladies make it back home. "Look Vanessa I got a movie want to watch it with me?"

"Sure what you got?"

“I found an oldie but goodie waiting to exhale.”

“That is one of my favorite movies, you get the DVD player ready and I will start dinner.” Tranetta talking from the living room

“So what are you cooking Vanessa?”

“I thought I would make my world famous Lasagna, buttered rolls and toss salad.”

“That sounds delicious, who taught you how to cook?”

“My Mom”

Tranetta was hesitant because there is a lot about her that Vanessa don’t know yet. There is a knock at the door.

"I wonder who this is. I'll get it Vanessa"

It's the dorm manager Ms. Felicia.

"Hey Ladies just checking to make sure everything is ok for you, I have to make my rounds every night at seven and eleven p.m. to make sure everyone is in tact. Are you guys getting settled in?"

"Oh yes mam we are about to have dinner and watch a movie." Says Tranetta. "That's good if you need anything; please feel free to let me know."

"Ok have a good night Ms. Felicia." Tranetta closes the door and continue setting up the DVD player for their movie.

"Dinner's ready come and get it."

Shouts Vanessa.

"This smells wonderful I can hardly wait to taste it."

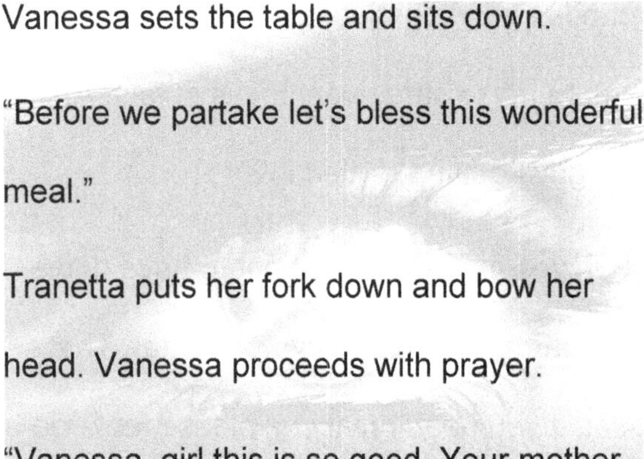

Vanessa sets the table and sits down.

"Before we partake let's bless this wonderful meal."

Tranetta puts her fork down and bow her head. Vanessa proceeds with prayer.

"Vanessa, girl this is so good. Your mother has taught you well."

"Thank you she loves to cook and thought us girls should at least know the basics."

"Girls how many sisters do you have?"

"Just one it's only my sister Tiffany and me. Do you have any sisters and brothers?"

"No it's just me an only child." So Vanessa what are you going to major in?" "First, I am going to become an R.N. then later go to medical school."

"That's Fascinating."

"So what are you going to do?"

"I'm not sure just taking some general classes right now."

Dinner is over; Vanessa clears the table and joins Tranetta in the living room for the movie. Vanessa is itching to get to that test so she can know for sure what is going on with her body. After the movie the girls chat for a while and decide to go to bed.

"Well, that will do it for me I have a get acquainted class tomorrow what are your plans Vanessa?"

"I have a class for whole campus rules at eight so I better get some sleep as well."

"Good night Vanessa." Tranetta is yawning as she heads for her bedroom. Vanessa quickly goes into her bedroom get the pregnancy test and goes into the bathroom lock the door and follow the directions carefully. After about three minutes the test stick turns blue for positive results. Vanessa sits on the bathroom floor and begins to sob like never before. Vanessa is terrified because she has no idea what happened that night or who she had sex with to get pregnant all her dreams of waiting until she find the right man to marry and have sex and a family with seem to be so far out of reach at this moment.

Vanessa wraps everything up carefully not to leave anything behind. She goes into her bedroom hide her evidence, get into bed and cry hysterically but quietly not to wake Tranetta.

"What am I going to do, no one will believe this, God help me get through this. Someone if not everyone knows what happened that night. Why are they not telling me, God help me please." Vanessa cries herself to sleep.

The next morning Tranetta is up bright and early making coffee and bagels.

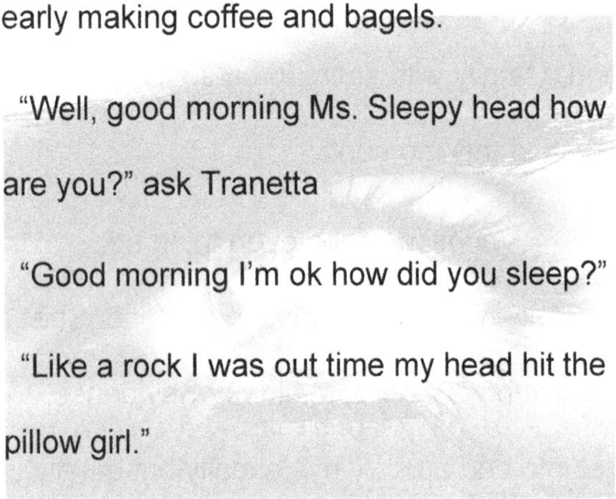

"Well, good morning Ms. Sleepy head how are you?" ask Tranetta

"Good morning I'm ok how did you sleep?"

"Like a rock I was out time my head hit the pillow girl."

Tranetta gives a little giggle as she grabs her bag to go.

"I'm out I will see you after class Vanessa there is coffee and bagels there for you."

"See you later have a good day."

Vanessa goes to the bathroom and throws up and sits on the floor hoping this is all just a bad dream. She slowly get up and shower, dresses and off to the first scheduled class.

"I need to call Jarvis and find out what happened."

As Vanessa is calling Jarvis she looks up and lo and behold Jarvis is walking into the student cafeteria.

"What is that J?"

Vanessa starts to walk fast so she can get a closer look and to her confirmation it's Jarvis.

"Jarvis, what are you doing here I thought you were going to school in Atlanta with Sheka."

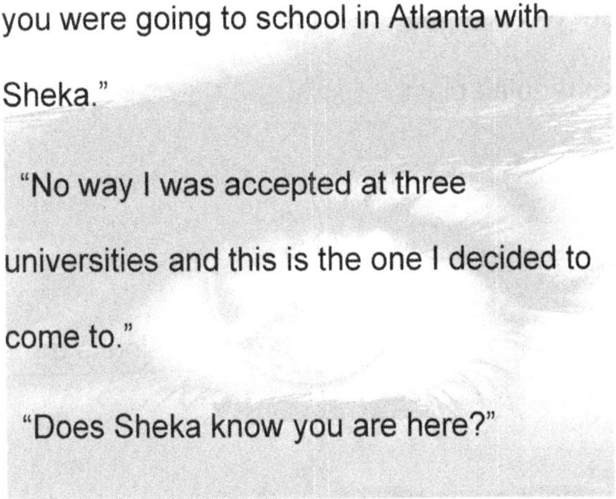

"No way I was accepted at three universities and this is the one I decided to come to."

"Does Sheka know you are here?"

"No and I would appreciate it if you didn't tell her I am through with her, are you ok Vanessa you look a little pale?"

"Yea, I just feel a little under the weather but I will be ok Jarvis I need you to be straight with me about that night at Sheka's party."

Jarvis looked as though he is scared to death.

"I would love to talk to you but it will have to be after class I'm late." Jarvis quickly walks away from Vanessa terrified.

"Jarvis, Jarvis meet me here after class." Vanessa rushes to the cafeteria after class waiting for an hour only to realize Jarvis is not going to show.

"I can't believe he didn't show." Just as Vanessa is about to leave Jarvis calls her from behind. "Jarvis I was getting worried."

"Why?"

"I thought you were avoiding me."

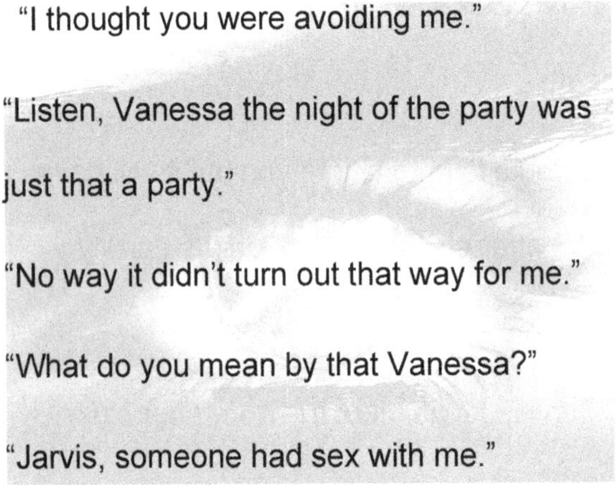

"Listen, Vanessa the night of the party was just that a party."

"No way it didn't turn out that way for me."

"What do you mean by that Vanessa?"

"Jarvis, someone had sex with me."

"What make you think that?"

"It's not what I think; the next morning I had semen in my panties Jarvis." Vanessa has tears coming down her face but does not tell

Jarvis she is pregnant, Jarvis feels so bad for Vanessa he grab her gently and hug her.

"Shh, it is going to be alright I wish that night would have never happened. Vanessa let me take you out to eat my treat ok."

"Not tonight I need to get back to the dorm I feel exhausted from today maybe this weekend."

"I think the weekend will be better I need to get my things unpacked and meet my new room mate. Let me walk you to your dorm."

"Ok"

As they are walking Jarvis tells Vanessa the reasons he broke up with

Sheka. They enter the dorm walk way and stop in front of Vanessa's room. "Thanks J for walking me home."

"No problem now I know where you are and plus I know you made it safe. Listen, Vanessa I really need to talk about some things with you when I see you on Saturday so be ready I will pick you about six ok."

'Ok J I will see you then."

Before Vanessa could open the door Tranetta opens the door fast

"Girl, I wasn't trying to be nosey but who is that? He is HOT." Jarvis is tall, medium brown skinned with a body that every woman would love to hold he is neat and very well dressed and as handsome as the movie star Shamar Moore.

"That is Jarvis we grew up together; I have known him since kindergarten." "Do all the brothers in Florida look like him?"

"You know I have never looked at him that way but, I guess he is kind of cute." "So Vanessa how was your day?'

"Girl, boring as hell that woman seem like she was never going to stop talking I can still hear her voice." They both laugh.

"So how was your day?"

"It was very, interesting"

"Yeah how interesting was it?"

"I met this guy from Chicago he wants to go out Saturday night but I'm not sure because he seems a little strange."

"Maybe you should follow your instincts."

"Maybe"

Vanessa is closely guarding her secret as she is contemplating between having a baby she has no idea how or who she got it from or to have an abortion. The thoughts of either are occupying her thoughts so deeply that she has not heard another word Tranetta is saying.

"Vanessa, Vanessa are you there?"

Tranetta snapping her fingers finally gets Vanessa's attention.

"Oh, I'm sorry Tranetta what did you say?"

"Girl you were in a trance are you ok?"

"Oh yeah I was just thinking about something my mom said to me."

"Anyway what would you like for dinner I stopped off and picked up a few things."

"I'm not hungry; I'll just grab a snack in a little while."

"Are you sure you're ok Vanessa you seem to be worried about something."

"I will be fine I think I'm going to go lay down for a while."

"Ok if you need me I will be here making some dinner."

Vanessa goes to her room and locks the door. "I am so confused God what should I do? If I have an abortion I can never forgive myself and if I have this baby I will have a lot of explaining to do about something I had no part in." Vanessa lies on the bed and curls up with a stuffed animal and cries herself to sleep once again.

It's Midnight and Vanessa is awakened by nausea, Vanessa walks into the living area and finds Tranetta knocked out on the sofa with an empty beer bottle in her hand.

"Tranetta wake up, Tranetta"

Tranetta groogy from sleeping awaken to Vanessa over her.

"I hear you girl, I must have fallen asleep."

"How many beers did you have?"

"Not enough, I wish I could get some Grey Goose and get loose"

"Tranetta girl you a mess come on let me help you to bed." They walk arm and arm to their bedrooms where they sleep until morning.

Saturday morning

Vanessa is up early feeling nauseated once again but seems to be in good spirits. Vanessa walks into the kitchen to find a mess Tranetta left before passing out, dishes everywhere, beer bottles, food on the stove, food on the floor Vanessa is thinking what a mess.

"I guess I better clean this mess, I can't stand a dirty kitchen or bathroom and Tranetta seems to be cool with being nasty,

I think I need to speak with her about this before it gets out of control." Little does Vanessa know Tranetta is not the perfect college girl she thinks. Tranetta comes from a totally different lifestyle than what Vanessa is used to. Tranetta mother threw her out when she was sixteen, never knew her father, she had to survive the streets by any means necessary. However, Tranetta did graduate and decided to use her scholarship in Volley ball to get a college degree, but she really just wants to find a rich man that will take care of her I guess you can call her a gold digger. Tranetta slowly walks into the kitchen where

Vanessa is fixing breakfast.

“Good morning Vanessa”

“Good morning Tranetta.”

“Sorry for the mess I meant to get to it but

seem to have fallen a sleep.”

“I guess you entitled to a mess up but try to

clean up behind yourself ok.

“Hey it’s Saturday and it’s date night.”

“Are you going out with the guy from

Chicago, what is his name anyway?’

“Yes I am and his name is Andre Williams, I

decided to go out with him because I hear

he got some big change.”

"So you're going out with him because he has money."

"Girl I can't hang with a brother unless he has money, broke is just a joke." Vanessa is kind of surprised to hear Tranetta speak this way.

"Tranetta money is not everything you need in a relationship."

"Really, well it is by my standards, I can't think of anything else worth letting some man breathe all in your face."

Vanessa is just looking at Tranetta as though she is an alien or something.

"Tranetta what was your life like before you came here to school?"

"Well, since you're asking I'll tell you, I didn't come from a fine two parent family, I had to do it the hard way, no one has ever made it easy for me so now I am taking some things for myself and getting a rich husband is one of those things I will take if you don't mind me saying so."

Vanessa is beginning to sense some things she doesn't quite like about Tranetta. "I better get a shower I want to go shopping and get some decorations for our little humble abode you know liven it up a bit."

"I guess you are the decorator Ms. Vanessa cause I can think of better things to spend money on but I guess when you have money to burn you have the tendency to waste it."

Vanessa is really beginning to feel another side of Tranetta. However, she just ignores her comments and leaves the room. Vanessa gets dressed and leaves for the shopping center without saying anything to Tranetta.

"Oh well, I don't know what her problem is spoiled brat!" Tranetta decides to snoop around in Vanessa's things.

"Well, look at this I bet this watch cost a bundle, I wonder what her daddy is like.. Probably one of those stuck up type business men who don't have a clue what a good fuck is, I bet her mom just likes it in one position. This little prissy BITCH! What else she got here with her little green ass." Tranetta continues to snoop and finds the pregnancy test Vanessa put in her trash. Tranetta takes it out and quickly goes to empty Vanessa trash as though she cleaned house.

Later that evening

"Tranetta are you home, I'm back I got some good stuff come see." But Tranetta has already left to go get into her own excitement.

"Hum, wonder where she went to, I don't know why I care that girl has issues. I think I may have to move if she don't straighten up her little attitude." Just as Vanessa is about to walk to the bedroom Jarvis knocks at the door.

"Who is it?"

"It's Jarvis.'

"Hey J I thought we weren't meeting until later in the evening?"

"That's why I'm here I was walking pass and decided to drop by and see if we are still on for tonight."

"Sure, about seven o'clock good."

"That's good so I will be back at seven so make sure you're ready I hate waiting, I'm just kidding, do you like Mexican."

"Yes I love Mexican" "good because I saw a nice Mexican restaurant just outside the campus about two blocks from here." Alright J as long as I am in by curfew it's cool."

"No problem I happen to have the same curfew."

"Right, so I'll see you then."

Vanessa starts hanging the pictures she brought earlier. Vanessa has a great eye for decorations.

"All done boy these decors really helped this place out." Vanessa has decorated the whole place in a matter of two hours. Vanessa looks at the beautiful wall clock and notices time has gotten away from her.

"I better get ready Jarvis will be here in thirty mins. What am I going to wear?" Vanessa whips her hair into an up do and dresses in a beautiful sky blue blouse with the earrings matching, a pair of baby Phat jeans with some sky blue stilettos. Jarvis is at the door looking like he just stepped out of fine men magazine and smelling like a million dollars. Jarvis parents own a strip mall, dance club, and a number of rental homes, so the boy has plenty of money in his account as well. “Look at you girl looking all fine you have always been a great dresser.”

“You look pretty fly yourself J not that you don’t always.”

They both look at one another for a quick second.

"Let me get my purse and we can be on our way." Jarvis opens the door for Vanessa to his fire red Porsche.

"This is a nice ride J when did you get this?"

"My dad bought it for me as a graduation gift nice huh?'

"Yea I really like it, I guess my dad will get me a new one but he says I have to prove myself first and then we will see what's up."

"I'm sure you will do great you always been very smart, on every committee you could find, you know how popular you are but of course I don't have to tell you that."

"I'm not so sure if I am popular anymore seems like after the party people started shying away from me and whispering about me. I'm still totally confused about that night and feel as though something terrible has happened to me." Jarvis pulls up for the valet to park his car and come around to walk Vanessa to the door of the restaurant.

"After you my dear."

"Thank you"

Vanessa and Jarvis are seated in a cozy booth with candles.

"This is nice J good call."

"I told you I know my restaurants."

"Well I will let you know once I taste the food."

Vanessa and Jarvis are having the time of their lives, Vanessa and Jarvis have been friends since Kindergarten when they met in Mrs. Hayworth class.

"So what you think of the food?"

"Jarvis I must say you know good food, that was delicious."

All of a sudden Vanessa is feeling very nauseated and just gets up without saying a word and run into the ladies room.

Everything comes up Vanessa just feels drained and wants to end her night with

Jarvis, Vanessa gets herself together splash some cold water on her and rinses her mouth out and walk back to the table.

“Vanessa are you alright?”

“I’m good can we leave I need to lay down my allergies are bothering me. Jarvis knowing what went down at the party is beginning to get suspicious about Vanessa’s allergies or so called allergies.

“Ok wait let me pay the tab and we will leave.” Jarvis pays for dinner and escorts Vanessa to the car. Jarvis walks Vanessa to the door to make sure she is safe.

"I had a wonderful time Jarvis thanks for being so kind."

"No problem we will do it again soon take care and get some rest I will call and check on you later."

"Good night J." Vanessa walks in and notices that Tranetta still has not returned and it's already eleven o'clock and curfew is midnight.

"I hope Tranetta makes curfew I would hate to see her get in trouble within her first week of school."

Ten minutes later Tranetta stumbles in drunk talking loud.

"HEY VANESSA GIRL, WHAT UP DOG!"

"Tranetta are you drunk?"

"I guess you could say that."

"Here let me help you to your room."

Vanessa takes Tranetta arm and throws it around her neck and coast Tranetta to her bed and lay her down Tranetta is out like a light. Vanessa closes her door and goes to bed as well.

Its six thirty Sunday morning and Vanessa is awakened by her cell phone and nausea on the other end is Sheka.

"Hey Sheka what's going on?"

Sheka is on the other end crying.

"Jarvis did not come to Atlanta, have you heard from him?"

Vanessa thinks back to Jarvis making her promise not to tell Sheka where he is but she also don't want to lie to her friend.

"No, I have not what's going on?"

"Jarvis is going to school somewhere else but his parents won't tell me where his Mother was really cold to me and now I am just hurt Jarvis just left me without a word."

"I'm sorry to hear this Sheka, I am sure Jarvis will call you when he is ready."

"I hope so I miss him so much."

"Sheka how is school coming along?"

“Its ok, I can’t concentrate right now without my Jarvis.”

“How is Texas?”

“I love it here the school is cool and my dorm is the bomb.”

“That’s good listen if you hear from Jarvis tell him to call me as soon as possible.” “I will”

“Well, I got to go Vanessa I will talk to you later.”

Before Vanessa could respond Sheka had already hung up.

“Wow, that’s crazy I need to let Jarvis know Sheka is tripping.”

Vanessa calls Jarvis but gets no answer and leaves him a voicemail to call her when he gets her message.

In the meantime, Tranetta stumbles up and goes into the bathroom and takes a shower. Vanessa is cleaning the living room when Tranetta comes out. "Good morning Vanessa."

"Good morning Tranetta."

"Hey Vanessa I want to apologize for my behavior yesterday I wasn't being nice and for that I apologize."

"Awe, its ok, so I take it you had a good time last night."

"Vanessa girl, Andre is so cool and handsome we had a great time."

'What year is he in here?"

"Oh no come to find out he has already graduated. When I met him in the library he was just doing some research he graduated four years ago and owns a fabulous club downtown."

"Wow he sounds exciting tell me more."

"He has a big home in the River oaks area where all these rich people stay. He has a five bedroom home, four bathrooms, two living rooms, three car garages and a swimming pool. I hit the jack pot girl."

"That's good I hope you two have a great relationship and maybe even get married."

"That's the plan, to hook him and get married and have two children with him. Did you go out with your date last night?"

"Yes Jarvis and I went to a beautiful Mexican restaurant just up the street; they have some really good food too."

"So how do you know this guy?"

"We grew up together we are just friends that's it."

"That's how it usually starts." The both laugh.

"I need to get dressed Andre is picking me up in an hour he wants me to ride to Dallas with him he has some stuff to pick up for the club. What you got planned for the day?"

"Nothing much, I think I will get some rest and get ready for class tomorrow."

Tranetta goes to dress for her date with Andre. Andre is right on time. outside of the dorm door blowing his horn for Tranetta to come out.

"Got to go see you later Vanessa smooches."

"Hey baby girl you looking fine."

"Thanks you too, but of course I don't think you could get any finer than you are right now."

"Flattery will get you everywhere."

They are zooming down the highway in Andre's black Cadillac enjoying the scene and one another. Finally, they reach their destination Andre pulls up to a big mansion. "This is my friend Russell house; I'll only be a few minutes so why don't you just hang out."

"Ok"

Andre goes in and does business with Russell who is a big drug dealer. Andre is not really an alumnus of the university he is a big drug dealer as well and has a wife and two children his wife and children are out of town visiting relatives for a month. Andre comes out and gets into the car and drives to a hotel.

"How about we stay here for tonight?"

"Well, you know I have curfew."

"That's right I forgot baby, well lets have some lunch and head back before dark that way I can steal you until eleven then take you home, will that work?'

"That's cool"

"Alright it's a bet.'

Andre and Tranetta have lunch and head back to Houston when they arrive in the city Andre takes Tranetta to his house where they spend the rest of the evening.

Its eleven thirty and Tranetta is singing as she walks into the dorm.

"Looks like you had a good time."

"Vanessa he is the one. What did you do?"

"Absolutely nothing"

"I'm beat I will see you in the morning before class so nighty, night Vanessa."

"Good night Tranetta"

Just as Vanessa is about to get into the shower her cell phone rings.

"Hey Vanessa its Jarvis I got your message, what's up?"

"Jarvis, I got a call from Sheka at six thirty this morning she was a mess. But I didn't tell her you were here, what's really going on with you two anyway?"

"I wish I could come over and talk to you right now but since its curfew can we meet before class in the morning I really need to talk to you."

"It sounds serious."

"It is so can we meet about seven in the cafeteria it opens at six."

"Ok I will see you then."

"Good night Vanessa."

"Good night Jarvis."

Now Vanessa is wondering again about the night of the party.

"I wonder what Jarvis have to tell me that is so important? Maybe he knows what happened and can clear this all up for me."

Vanessa is also seriously thinking about having an abortion because she can't see herself having a baby by someone she has no idea who that person is.

Six a.m.

Vanessa is up and ready to find out what Jarvis is so serious about. Vanessa gets up and gets a cup of hot tea and wait until its time to walk to the cafeteria. While she is waiting Tranetta comes into the kitchen and join her for a cup of tea. After some conversation with Tranetta its time for Vanessa to leave, Vanessa grabs her things say her good day to Tranetta and out the door to the cafeteria. Jarvis is already there waiting. When Jarvis sees Vanessa he stands and gives her a hug and pulls her chair out for her to sit. Jarvis is nervous because he doesn't know how Vanessa is going to take what he has to tell her. "Would you like something to eat Vanessa?"

"No I would like a cup of peppermint tea though."

"One cup of peppermint tea coming up"

Jarvis walks over to the counter and order Vanessa tea and him a croissant and small coffee.

"Here you go a hot cup of tea for the lady."

"Thanks J this smells better than mine, maybe I'm not doing something right." Jarvis takes a sip of his coffee.

"Vanessa, we have been friends for a long time, you are a good person and I hope that we can always remain the best of friends."

Vanessa sees how nervous Jarvis is.

"Jarvis what is it?"

"Vanessa I feel so bad about the night of the graduation party at Sheka's. Sheka is not your friend; she put alcohol in the punch to get you drunk. When you passed out I helped her take you to her room and while you were asleep some more friends came to the party and went in the room where you were. Sheka and I argued because I was trying to stop them from going in there and she just was tripping. I finally decided to go into the room and found you completely out of it and they had sex with you." Vanessa is in shock because Odell's friends had sex with her Odell was just there he didn't get a chance because Jarvis came in and threw them out. Vanessa sits in shock with tears rolling down her face still not knowing her cousin Odell was the ring leader. She can't move or speak its like she has become a stone wall.

"Vanessa say something please, you got to know I didn't want that and had a fight with the one guy Jermaine that was getting off you."

Jarvis is now in tears as well.

"That's why I broke up with Sheka because she let it happen and I can't stand her and never want to see her again."

No matter what Jarvis says to Vanessa she is just sitting there with tears flowing down her cheeks which is breaking Jarvis heart. Finally Vanessa just gets up very slow and walks away like she is a zombie. Jarvis walks her home and opens her door for her. Once inside she lays on the couch where Vanessa curls up and cries profusely. Jarvis cries with her but will not leave her side. Vanessa's cell phone is ringing and its Sheka but Vanessa don't answer. Jarvis kneels down beside Vanessa as she lay in endless tears.

"Vanessa I am so sorry. I don't ever want anyone to ever hurt you this way again." Vanessa sits up on the sofa and look deeply into Jarvis eyes with so much pain in her heart.

"Jarvis you don't understand I am pregnant and don't know who has fathered this child. Who is this Jermaine guy anyway I need to get to his ass" Jarvis face goes white as though all the blood has drained out of his body.

"Oh my God, Vanessa I am so sorry."

"What am I going to do Jarvis? I am so angry, hurt, betrayed and shame. I can't have this baby. who were they Jarvis TELL ME WHO RAPED ME."

Vanessa screaming at Jarvis

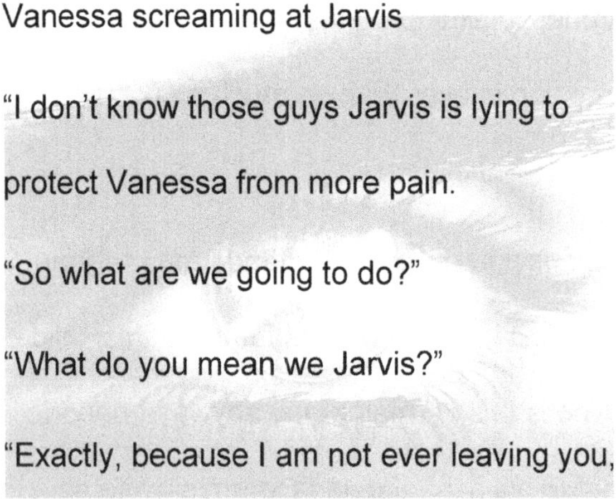

"I don't know those guys Jarvis is lying to protect Vanessa from more pain.

"So what are we going to do?"

"What do you mean we Jarvis?"

"Exactly, because I am not ever leaving you, Vanessa its time that I tell you how I have felt for years, I love you always have. I am asking you to give me a chance to help you through this and to allow me to be the man you want and need." "Jarvis right now I am so confused that I don't know who I am right now I need some time to think about this."

"Well in the meantime can I get you anything? A drink, something to eat"

"No, but right now I would like to be alone to think about some things."

"Are you sure you're going to be alright?"

"No I'm not sure, Jarvis those bastards violated me and stole my virginity, my innocence something I was hoping to share with my husband. I don't know how I can be alright with that."

Vanessa falls into Jarvis arms and begin to cry profusely once again.

"Vanessa its ok calm down you are going to make yourself sick I can't leave you like this."

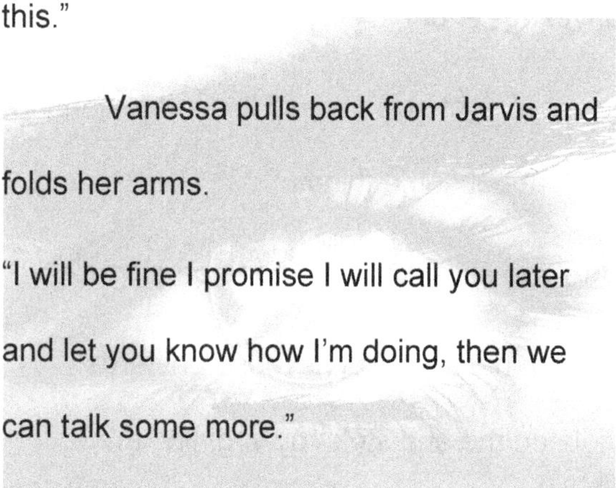

Vanessa pulls back from Jarvis and folds her arms.

"I will be fine I promise I will call you later and let you know how I'm doing, then we can talk some more."

"Promise"

"I promise."

"Ok call me if you need me to come back my phone will be right here ok." Vanessa walks Jarvis to the door and goes back to lie on the sofa just staring at the ceiling wondering what her parents would think of her. Vanessa feels like her whole world has crashed and she is in a bad dream and can't seem to wake up. Vanessa calls her mother.

"Hi mama"

"Hey Vanessa I thought you would be in class by now."

"I did we were just going over the syllabus."

"I am so proud of you, Tiffany can't stop talking about her big sister to all her friends she is just as proud of you as we are."

"I just wanted to hear your voice mom tell daddy I love him and I will talk to you soon."

"Ok baby do you need anything. Vanessa you sound like something is wrong, are you ok?"

"No I am fine, thanks mom talk to you later."

"Vanessa I love you if you need me just call you can talk to me about anything ok baby."

"I know I can I'll remember that Love you too mom."

Vanessa hangs up from her mom and get on her computer and look up abortion clinics. Vanessa calls an abortion clinic downtown and makes an appointment for the next day.

Tranetta enters in a hurry she has a big date with her man Andre.

"Vanessa I won't be here I need to get showered and out Andre is taking me to the game tonight. I also am pledging for the Deltas do you want to pledge with me?"

"Not now maybe later I'm busy with another project right now."

"Girl what could be more important than pledging for the Deltas do you know they are the largest African-American sorority there is?"

"Yes I know my mother is Delta and my dad is an Alpha man."

"Then what's the problem Vanessa your mom will expect this of you."

"Ok I'll think about it."

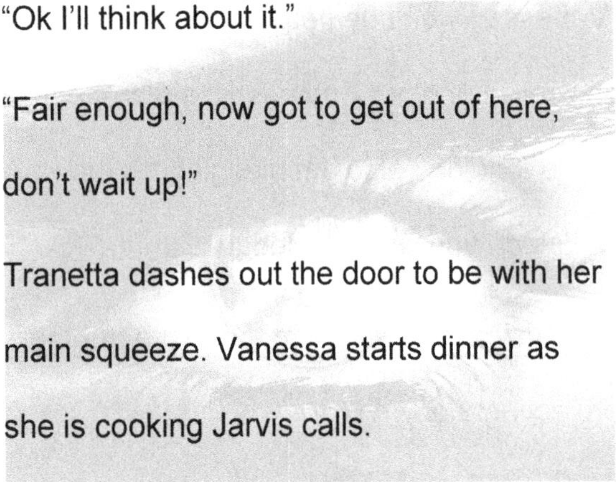

"Fair enough, now got to get out of here, don't wait up!"

Tranetta dashes out the door to be with her main squeeze. Vanessa starts dinner as she is cooking Jarvis calls.

"Vanessa are you alright?"

"Yea I'm good"

"Are you sure?"

"Yes J I am, hey how about you come over and have some dinner with me I am making some chicken, mashed potatoes and a salad."

"Cool I'm on my way."

Jarvis is excited about tasting Vanessa's cooking, he has been attracted to Vanessa since grade school and don't know what made him choose Sheka over her. Jarvis is knocking at the door before Vanessa could hang the phone up. "Man when you said you would be right over you weren't kidding."

"Girl a home cooked meal you better know it and it smells good too."

"Make your self at home while I put the finishing touches to dinner."

Jarvis is talking to Vanessa from the living room.

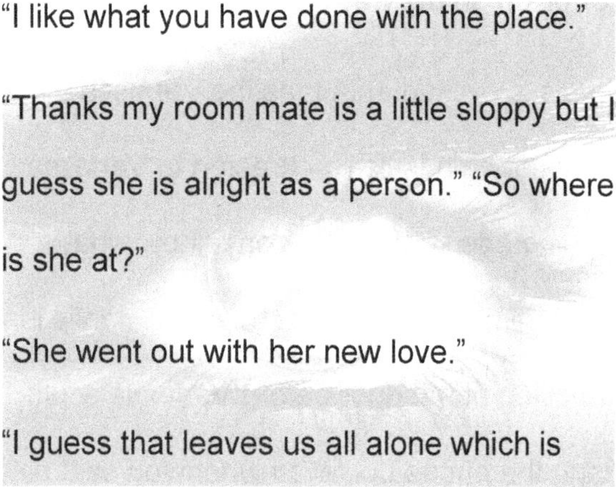

"I like what you have done with the place."

"Thanks my room mate is a little sloppy but I guess she is alright as a person." "So where is she at?"

"She went out with her new love."

"I guess that leaves us all alone which is good."

"Yes it is because I need to talk to you without people around anyway."

Jarvis moves to the table to get closer as Vanessa is setting the table. "Boy this looks great Vanessa."

"Let me say grace."

Vanessa gives thanks for the meal and Jarvis dig in.

"Girl this is delicious where did you learn how to cook like this? You got this food seasoned to perfection."

"You know my mama she had to teach us girls how to cook; you know they say a way to a man's heart is to feed him."

"That's a true saying however, you caught my heart just being you."

"Jarvis, I made an appointment for tomorrow morning to have an abortion."

Jarvis stops eating and leans back in his seat.

"Vanessa, wow, are you sure?"

"I can't have this baby, all my dreams will be gone and not to think how embarrassed my family will be."

"Man, I can't let you go alone, Vanessa I want to be with you and share everything with you. Can I be that man that will be there for you?"

"I can't think about a relationship right now, oh by the way Sheka called me but I didn't answer her I am so angry with her that I know I will lose it and cuss her out so to avoid all that right now I just don't even want to speak to her."

"She has some issues and I don't care to speak to her either, she definitely was not right for me. She really surprised me how she treated you the night of this craziness. Sheka had everybody there banned from speaking to you."

"How many people were there?"

"Most of the crowd was gone so it was about seven people left just hanging out."

After dinner Jarvis helps Vanessa clean the dishes, then they moved to the living room to talk some more.

“Jarvis, thank you for being here with me and I must admit that I always had a crush on you as well but Sheka came along so aggressive that she just over shadowed me.”

“I wish that hadn’t happened she is like dirt to me know, but enough about Sheka, I want you to get some rest so you can be ready for tomorrow. What time is your appointment?”

“Nine o’clock”

"Cool, I better get out of here I will pick you up at eight."

Vanessa walks Jarvis to the door and gives him a big hug.

"Good night Jarvis see you at eight."

Tranetta comes in with bags and a big smile.

"Vanessa come see what my man bought me girl."

"Looks like he bought the whole mall look at all this stuff."

"Vanessa girl I am so happy he is so good to me."

"I'm happy for you, we all need somebody to love and care for us and I am glad you found that someone."

They hug and Tranetta takes her things into her bedroom and close her door for the night leaving Vanessa to think about her big day in the morning.

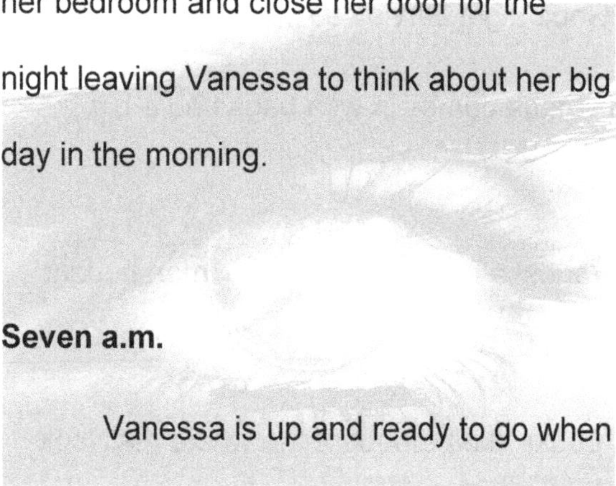

Seven a.m.

Vanessa is up and ready to go when Jarvis comes by to pick her up. "Ready Nessa?"

"As ready as I will ever be come on let's go before Tranetta gets up I don't want her to know my business." They arrive at the abortion clinic and Vanessa gets a chill up her spine at the thought of having to do this.

"Vanessa are you ok? You know you don't have to do this."

"Let me just have a minute to get myself together I will be alright."

"Vanessa I have been thinking, if this is too much for you, I mean we can get through this if you decide not to go through with this."

"Exactly what do you mean by that Jarvis because I don't know how we can get through this I am pregnant in case you forgot and it happens to be somebody baby who I have no idea who. Now you tell me how we fix THAT, and besides I am in school and I still have to face my parents and the world."

"Please Vanessa I didn't mean to upset you I am just giving you another alternative if you would just hear me out."

"Right now I just want to get this over with so please, if you want to help me let's just go ok."

Jarvis backs down and opens Vanessa's door and they go into the abortion clinic.

The receptionist is warm and friendly.

"Good morning do you have an appointment?"

"Yes I have a nine o'clock, my name is Vanessa Carter."

"Yes Ms. Carter fill out the forms and when you are finished brings them back and have a seat ok."

Vanessa takes the forms and begins filling them out as Jarvis is looking around. After about an hour the nurse calls Vanessa back, Vanessa follows the nurse to an exam room where she is told to strip from the waist down. Vanessa is terrified at the unknown and the room seems so gloomy.

"Oh, what am I doing I can't do this."

Vanessa grabs her clothes dresses and runs out of the exam room passing the nurse.

"Ms. Carter where are you going?"

"I'm sorry I can't do it I'm sorry."

Vanessa dashes out the door to the waiting room and grabs Jarvis by the hand.

"Vanessa what's wrong?"

"Just come on let's go let's just go please."

When they get in the car Vanessa is sobbing uncontrollably and Jarvis is trying to comfort as best as he can. "Vanessa I know you're hurt but this can be rectified if you would just let me help you. Have you thought about what I asked you?"

"How can I think about being in a relationship right now with so much going on?" "If you would let me love you I promise to make this all better and give you and the baby a good life."

"Even though I am carrying a baby that we don't know who it belongs to?"

"Yes, Vanessa I care about you that much, I know what kind of person you are and none of this is your fault and besides when a person loves someone those things don't matter."

"Jarvis are you sure you want to be involved in this?"

"I am more than sure I am positive and will be by your side to help you every step of the way." Jarvis lifts Vanessa's chin softly and lean in to kiss her. Vanessa is absorbed in Jarvis sweet, soft full lips that she is not crying anymore its like Jarvis kiss has taken every pain away. Jarvis pulls away gently and looks deeply into Vanessa's eyes. Vanessa is fully entrusted by Jarvis kiss and begin to realize how sexy he really is. Jarvis starts the car and drive away from the abortion clinic.

"Vanessa, first we need to get you and me both to class and after class is over we can get some dinner and discuss our plans about how we want to handle the relationship ok."

"Ok Jarvis, Jarvis I really do appreciate you being such a good friend all these years and especially now. I do have to admit that I have always had a bad crush on you too."

"See I knew it, now we can fulfill how we feel about one another oh and I planned to come to school here the whole time, you didn't think I was going to let you get away from me did you?" they both laugh and Vanessa is finally feeling much better knowing that she has someone who cares about her to help her in the troublesome time.

Jarvis pulls up to a parking space at the school.

"Here we are, ready, oh Vanessa don't worry about nothing I got you."

Vanessa is walking into the building and looks back at Jarvis; he blows a kiss her way. Vanessa is all smiles as she walks to her class thinking how blessed she is and how she will be a good woman for Jarvis and her baby. As Vanessa is about to walk into her class she hears Tranetta calling her.

"Vanessa wait a minute. Girl where you been? I woke up looking for you and you were gone.'

"I met Jarvis for breakfast."

"Looks like somebody got them a dude."

"We are getting close, listen Tranetta I will talk to you later I need to get in this class before I miss the whole lecture."

"Ok I'll see you at home."

Class is over and Jarvis is anxious to see Vanessa when he runs into Odell. "Jarvis, man what you doing here?" Jarvis don't feel too friendly towards Odell. "I'm going to school do you mind?"

“I’m just surprised to see you. I thought maybe you would be attending school somewhere else.”

“Well I’m here and if you would excuse me I’m late.”

“Alright dude I’ll see you around.’

Jarvis is furious he thought Odell went to another school in Texas.

“Dam, he must have transferred I can’t let Vanessa know it was Odell in that room that night.”

Jarvis is feeling afraid because he does not want Vanessa to know Odell is one of the main culprits to this whole nightmare.

Vanessa is feeling good for the first time in weeks as she is getting ready to shower her phone rings and its sheka.

"Hello"

"Hey Nessa girl what you doing?"

Vanessa wants to confront her but decides not to at this time. However, she is short with her.

"Nothing"

"So have you heard from Jarvis?"

"No"

"Vanessa is something wrong?"

"I have to go I'll talk to you later."

Vanessa hung up in Sheka's face. Sheka is a little puzzled.

"What was that about?"

Sheka mumbles to herself, looking at her phone at the same time. Vanessa is disturbed by Sheka phone call.

"The nerve of that BITCH, I'm not finished with her I will see her again."

Tranetta rushes in passing Vanessa like she running from the police.

"Hey Vanessa, I'm late got to meet Andre we are going to the movies and I need to get changed and out."

Vanessa is talking to Tranetta from the kitchen.

"Boy, you and Mr. Andre really hitting it off huh?"

Tranetta flies back pass Vanessa as she is running to the door.

"Ok don't wait up be back before curfew."

Vanessa shakes her head with a smile and go in for a long hot bath. Jarvis calls while Vanessa is bathing.

"Hello beautiful are you busy?"

"I'm just taking a hot bath."

"That sounds very intriguing. I wish I was the soap."

Vanessa gives a little giggle.

‘Well, Mr. J how about you come by and we catch a movie and snuggle, would you like that?”

“I’ll be there in an hour.”

“Ok see you then.”

They hang up and Jarvis is smiling like he won the lotto. Vanessa finishes her bath and puts on a big T shirt, wraps her hair and start looking through the DVD’s. Vanessa makes her selections goes to the kitchen and puts some popcorn in the microwave.

Jarvis is at the door with a big smile and his hands behind his back.

“Hey girl, I brought you something.” Jarvis brings the flowers from behind him and hold up a dozen of long stem yellow roses.

“These are for you my love.’

“Oh, this is so sweet, come in I popped us some popcorn and I put in a movie.” Vanessa turns around and Jarvis is right there and gently grab Vanessa and lays a sweet tender kiss upon her lips. Jarvis takes Vanessa by the hand and lead her to the living room so they can snuggle and watch a movie. Vanessa is lying in Jarvis lap when she starts to cry.

"Vanessa are you crying."

"Yes"

"why"

"Because I am happy and scared all at the same time." Jarvis raise Vanessa from his lap and put his arm around her and pulls her close.

"Baby, you don't have to feel afraid anymore I am right here and I got you. I feel all my dreams are coming true and the most important part of my dream is you. I want you to be happy and I will spend every day trying to fulfill your dreams." "Thank you J I am still afraid of one thing and that's my parents, what am I going to tell them?"

"Lets give it a few months, first, we have to tell our parents we are seeing each other and then take it from there."

"Ok"

"Well, it time for my curfew I better get out of here." Jarvis gives Vanessa a kiss and dashes out the door. Tranetta passes Jarvis as she is coming up the walkway. Odell is running trying to catch curfew and runs into Tranetta knocking her down.

"Hey watch where you going!" Odell just keeps running, Tranetta gets up and dust herself off and walk into the dorm just in time. Vanessa is already in bed when Tranetta comes in; Tranetta gets a cold drink and off to bed. Vanessa is lying in bed but does not get up to talk to Tranetta she just wants to sleep.

It's been four months and school is going well, Vanessa and Jarvis are getting closer. However, things are going a little sour for Tranetta. Andre has not called her in a week. Tranetta has been calling him everyday and every minute on the hour. Tranetta is worried about Andre and takes a bus to his home, upon her arrival she see a woman and two children with Andre close behind as they get into a Mercedes Benz and drive away. Tranetta heart is pounding as the tears roll down her face it seems as though they are burning tattoos into her cheeks. "Maybe it's not what I think. Maybe that's his sister, yea that's probably a relative." Tranetta gets herself together and goes back to the campus. Tranetta gets back to the campus and goes to the student lounge and gives Andre another call this time Andre answers.

"What up"

"Hey it's me Tranetta or have you forgotten me already?"

"No, what you need?"

"Andre what's going on?"

"What you mean?"

"Well, you haven't answered any of my calls and now you seem to be so cold." "Listen, I got to go I'll hit you back later." Andre hangs up in Tranetta's face; Tranetta is feeling so low at this point wondering who the woman and children are that she saw Andre with earlier. Tranetta is walking back to the dorm when she bumps into Odell again.

"You the one knocked me down last night.

"Sorry I was in a rush to make curfew, let me properly introduce myself I'm Odell."

"I'm Tranetta nice to meet you now if you don't mind getting out of my way I would like to get to where I'm going without knocking you down."

"Oh, we got jokes, ok Ms. Tranetta I guess I'll see you around with your fine self." Tranetta just gives him a snarl and walk away.

"What's up Tranetta?"

"Not a whole lot."

"What's wrong you seem so down lately are you ok, would you like to talk about it?"

"Not really" Tranetta just walks back to her bedroom. Sheka is calling Vanessa again.

"Hello"

"Hey Nessa what you doing girl?"

"I'm getting ready to do some laundry."

"Why you acting all dry with me?" "I'm not dry with you I'm just busy Sheka."

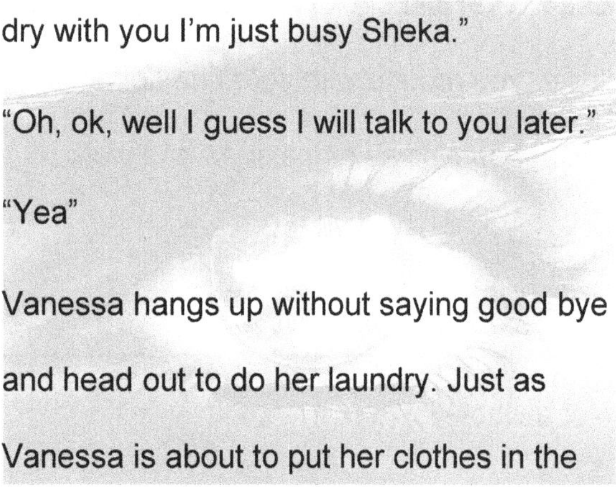

"Oh, ok, well I guess I will talk to you later."

"Yea"

Vanessa hangs up without saying good bye and head out to do her laundry. Just as Vanessa is about to put her clothes in the washer her father Terry calls.

"Hey baby how is Daddy's little girl?"

"Hey Daddy I am good I'm doing my laundry, so how is Mom and Tiffy doing?"

"Everybody is good, do you need anything?"

"No I'm good."

"So how is school coming along?"

"Very well Daddy I really like it here."

"That's great baby, I was just calling to hear your voice we all miss you and love you."

"I miss you too and love you very much."

"Well, I'll let you get back to your laundry and we will see you for Thanksgiving ok."

"Ok Daddy love you bye."

Vanessa is feeling so good she is not feeling all the morning sickness so much anymore. Vanessa is taking her clothes out the washer to put them in the dryer when her phone rings again this time it's her boo Jarvis.

"Hello sweet love of my life."

"Hey baby, with your fine self."

"What do I owe the pleasure of this call?"

"I want to know if you would like to go see this play that's in town this evening."

"I love stage plays Jarvis what time does it start?"

"Eight"

"I'll be ready at seven."

"Bet I'll pick you up at seven."

"Ok baby see you then bye."

Vanessa can hardly wait to see this play. Vanessa quickly finishes her laundry and head back to the dorm, on her way she sees Odell from a distance. "I must be dreaming is that my cousin Odell? Vanessa walks closer to make sure.

"Odell"

Odell turns around and to his surprise and fright it's Vanessa

"Hey cuz, I didn't know you were here."

"Yea I'm taking classes here, what are you doing here I thought you were going to school in another part of Texas?"

"I was but I transferred here to be closer to home."

Vanessa is happy to see someone from her family.

"Hey Odell how about we grab some lunch sometime?"

Odell is nervous from seeing Vanessa and wants to run away.

"Ok maybe you know right now my schedule is pretty full."

"Ok when you get time just let me know and we can hang out."

"I got to get out of here so I will see you around cuz." Odell takes off like he running from the police.

Vanessa walks to the dorm to get ready for her date with Jarvis.

"Hey anybody home?"

no one answers Tranetta has already left. Vanessa puts her laundry up and starts getting ready for her date. Its six o'clock when Tranetta comes in with an attitude because she is having problems communicating with Andre.

“What’s up Tranetta, girl Jarvis is taking me to the theater tonight to see a play that’s in town.”

“Great”

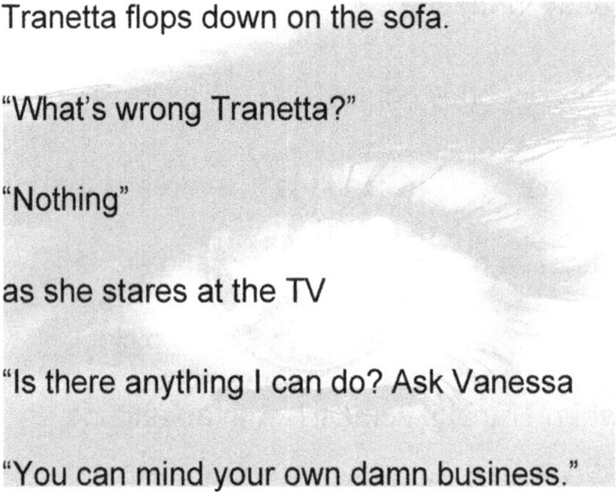

Tranetta flops down on the sofa.

“What’s wrong Tranetta?”

“Nothing”

as she stares at the TV

“Is there anything I can do? Ask Vanessa

“You can mind your own damn business.”

Tranetta rushes pass Vanessa go to her room and slams the door.

"Man, what's her problem?" Vanessa whispers to herself.

Vanessa finishes dressing and wait for Jarvis. Its seven o'clock and Jarvis is right on time.

"Hey J you look great."

"I must say Vanessa you are stunning as always."

"Thank you Jarvis I really enjoyed the show."

"It was a good show."

"Would you like to come in for a quick snack J?"

"Sure"

Vanessa walks into the kitchen to prepare a snack when Jarvis comes up behind her and start to kiss her on the neck. Vanessa turns around and returns the love Vanessa takes Jarvis by the hand and led him to her bedroom.

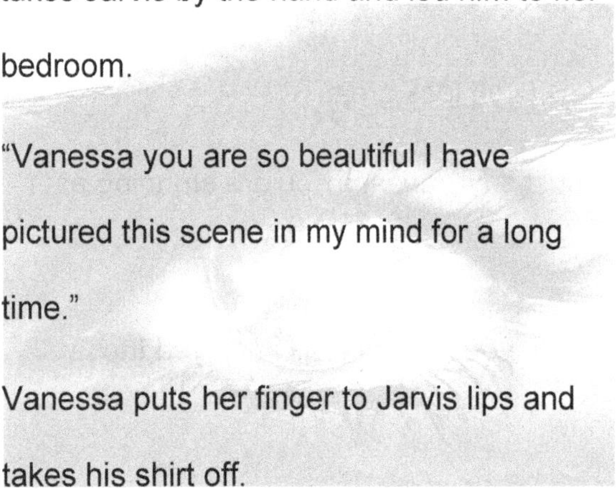

"Vanessa you are so beautiful I have pictured this scene in my mind for a long time."

Vanessa puts her finger to Jarvis lips and takes his shirt off.

"Vanessa are you sure I don't want to rush you."

Vanessa still silent stands before Jarvis and strips. Jarvis eyes are engaged on Vanessa's shapely body. Jarvis takes his pants off to show his manhood which is more than Vanessa expected but she is delighted to see he has a good weapon. Jarvis reaches over Vanessa and turns on some music and put on a condom. Their bodies are engaged in a sea of lust as they thrust against one another with sweet passionate love.

Tranetta is up going to the bathroom when she notices sweet moans coming from Vanessa's room. Tranetta presses her ear to the door and listen as they explode with their love. Tranetta is feeling jealous and decides to quietly go back to her room. It's almost eleven and Jarvis has to leave but promises Vanessa he will see her tomorrow they kiss and Jarvis leaves. The next morning Tranetta is up making breakfast when Vanessa comes into the kitchen. "Good morning Tranetta" Vanessa feeling good after a night of love. Tranetta totally ignores Vanessa and walks pass her as though she is not standing there and goes to her room and closes the door. "What is her problem?" Vanessa wonders to herself.

Tranetta's phone rings and its Andre.

"Tranetta forgive me for being so short with you I have been so busy. I want to see you, can you see me today?"

"Andre, you just now calling me after you treated me so coldly yesterday what your girlfriend dumped you?"

"What are you talking about?"

"Nothing when you want to meet?"

"That's my girl I am going to make it up to you with a big surprise can you be ready in an hour?"

"I guess and you better not be late."

"Ok baby I will get you in an hour."

Tranetta finish her breakfast and rushes to get dressed, she is a fool for Andre. However, Tranetta have motives to get some of Andre's money and be his number one woman. Tranetta rushes out the door and leaves without saying a word to Vanessa. Vanessa just ignores her and decides to clean up. As she is cleaning Jarvis comes by

"Jarvis I wasn't expecting you so early."

"Forgive me but I had to see you girl. You put it on a brother last night and now you not going to be able to get rid of me."

Vanessa laughs

"Have a seat silly I will be right back."

Vanessa returns and sits with Jarvis on the sofa.

"Hey I almost forgot I saw my cousin Odell yesterday he is going to school here now."

Jarvis blood went cold just at the mention of Odell's name.

"Really, I thought he was in school somewhere else."

"He was and decided to transfer here to be closer to home."

"Vanessa listen we need to talk about what we are going to do about keeping the pregnancy silent."

"You know Jarvis since we have been together I just seem to have not paid much attention."

"Sorry to be a drag but we are going to have to do something."

"You're right but can we talk about it later? Right now I just want to snuggle in your arms." Once again they are thrust into the ocean of love. Tranetta and Andre are at the movies enjoying each other company. After the movies Andre and Tranetta is walking hand in hand when Tranetta decides to ask

Andre about the woman and children she saw him with.

"Andre, who is the woman and children I saw you with yesterday?"

"You saw me where?"

"I was coming to see you because you were not answering my calls I was worried and came by but when I got close to your house I saw you getting into a car with a woman and children."

"Girl you should have said something that is my sister and her kids I was taking them to the museum." Of course Andre is lying and quietly wants to hit Tranetta for coming by without calling. Andre phone rings and it's his wife.

"Tranetta baby I got some things going on I'm going to have to drop you off and when I'm finished I'll call you.

"Is everything alright?"

"Oh yea nothing I can't handle." Andre walks around and opens the door for Tranetta gives her a peck on the cheek and get back in his car and drives away in a hurry. Tranetta is somewhat disappointed. Tranetta walks into the apartment and find Vanessa and Jarvis snuggling on the couch. Tranetta just gives Vanessa and Jarvis a smirk and go to her bedroom. Jarvis is a little thrown by Tranetta's attitude.

"So what's the story on your girl?"

"I'm not sure for the last few days she has this attitude and I have no idea why I haven't done anything to her."

"Listen Vanessa I know you wanted to wait to talk about the situation with the baby but, I need to say something to you now. We love each other right? Well, I am thinking you are going to be showing with your pregnancy soon and of course your family is going to want to see you for the holidays. Well, Vanessa I think we should get married and move into a home we can still finish school and give the baby a good start."

"Jarvis, what would we do about money?"

"Baby, I have plenty of money my grand parents left me well off. I am going to school for my own personal growth money is not a problem and I am willing to share the fortune with you."

Tranetta over hear Jarvis plea to Vanessa but what really stands out in her mind is the word plenty of MONEY.

"Jarvis this is so sudden I will have to think about this."

"Ok baby I'm not going to force you but I do want you to know that I love you always have and I want to be with you and make a life for you and the baby ok." Tranetta mouth drops knowing Vanessa is pregnant this could be good for her. She has heard all she needs to know so she tip toe back to her room and start calculating some devious ways.

"I better get out of here but I do want you to think about it and when you are ready we can discuss this farther ok baby."

"Ok J I will give it a lot of thought, I'll see you tomorrow."

Jarvis gives vanessa a kiss and leaves.

Vanessa cleans the living room and as she is cleaning Tranetta walks out and stands by the doorway to the kitchen just looking at Vanessa.

"So your man left?"

"Oh are we talking to me now?"

Tranetta comes up with a sob story to get back in Vanessa's grace so she can use her for her own selfish motives.

"Vanessa, I have really been going through some crazy shit the last week and I had no right taking it out on you please forgive me for being a bitch I promise it won't happen again."

"Tranetta I want you to know you can talk to me about anything. Of course I forgive you."

"Thanks Vanessa this means a lot to me, I will get it together soon."

"So what's the problem?"

"It will be ok it's not anything I can't work out if it gets too over bearing you'll be the first to know."

"I'm here if you need me Tranetta but right now my bed is calling me so I will see you in the morning."

"Good night Vanessa sleep tight don't let the bed bugs bite."

Tranetta is scheming and trying to figure out how she can set somebody up to get paid. Her first set up begins with Andre.

Two weeks later

Jarvis is planning a sweet night of romance with Vanessa candles, soft music, dinner and a beautiful proposal. Jarvis has rented a room at the Marriot with full room service to surprise Vanessa.

"Jarvis you are so sneaky, where are you taking me?"

"Shh, it's a surprise now step up and let me lead you." Jarvis has Vanessa blindfolded and opens the door to the room and the scene is breath taking with long stem roses the smell of a delicious dinner of Steak and Lobster. Soft music is playing in the background. Jarvis stands Vanessa before the table and takes off the blind fold before her on the table is a black box with a two carat princess cut diamond ring.

"Oh my God Jarvis everything is so beautiful. You did this for me?" Vanessa starts to cry.

"Baby why are you crying, this is just a sample of what's to come."

Vanessa sits down and Jarvis kneels down in front of her and opens the black box. Vanessa gasps and places her hands to her mouth and cries even more. "Vanessa, will you be my wife?'

Vanessa is so excited she could not speak all she can do is cry and shake her head yes.

"You mean it Vanessa you will marry me?"

"Yes, I will"

Jarvis is so excited he stands Vanessa up and picks her up and swings her around with joy.

"There's more"

"What you mean more than this?"

"Yes"

"well what could be more than this beautiful scene?"

"I bought us a house in a beautiful neighborhood, the closing is in two weeks are you ready to do this Vanessa?"

"Jarvis I feel like I'm dreaming."

"No baby it's real sit let's eat before our food gets cold."

Jarvis and Vanessa are both swimming in a sea of happiness ending their night with lovemaking.

Tranetta is furious because she has not heard from Andre and decides to go to his house. Tranetta is going to make Andre pay for how he is treating her. Tranetta rings the door bell but no one answers. She is crying and exhausted from dealing with Andre. She is walking back to the campus when Odell pulls up and ask her if she needs a ride.

"Hey cutie pie remember me?"

"How can I forget you Mr. Mack daddy."

"Come on girl get in I'll give you a ride back to the dorm."

Tranetta kind of look at Odell funny but decides to take the ride.

"Don't try any funny stuff cause I don't want to have to kick your ass."

Odell just laughs and drives to the dorm. Vanessa and Jarvis are back and are in the living room when Odell and Tranetta walk in. Jarvis almost have a heart attack when he sees Odell walk in.

"Hey everybody, this is Odell, Odell this is my room mate Vanessa and her friend Jarvis."

"Odell what's up cuz?"

"Oh so you know each other?"

"Yea girl Odell is my cousin and he and Jarvis are cool too." Vanessa is all smiles. "So what's up with ya Jarvis man?"

"Not much just about to leave."

Jarvis is pissed and wants to take Vanessa as fast as he can and get out of there. Tranetta is really scheming now.

"Oh Vanessa you and Jarvis don't have to leave Odell and I can go to my room and listen to music. Odell is game for that because all he wants to do is hit it anyway.

"Hold up a minute Tranetta, J can I speak to you outside for a minute?"

"Yea I guess"

They step outside the door and Odell is curious.

"You haven't said anything to Vanessa about that night have you?"

"No and I don't plan to as long as you stay the fuck away from her."

"Jarvis thanks man let's just let this shit ride."

"You don't worry about that, I got it covered. You should be glad nigga cause you and your punk ass friends should be sitting in jail right now."

"Man, calm down I am thankful and I am going to stay away from Vanessa it's just hello and goodbye for me."

"Ok then it's settled."

They go back in and Jarvis wants Vanessa to go with him because he cannot trust Odell.

"Well Tranetta, Odell looks like you guys got the place to yourselves for a couple of hours I'll be back before curfew Tranetta see ya."

Vanessa and Jarvis leaves and go for a ride.

"So Ms. Tranetta what's the deal on you?"

"I'm just trying to get my education on and see where it takes me."

"What's your major?'

"Not sure yet, would you like a beer Odell?"

"That's what's up"

"So what's up with you Odell?"

"Same thing only I'm almost done with this shit. I'm an engineer major."

"Got a girlfriend?"

"Nope where's your man?"

"Don't have one."

Odell whips out a joint

"Want to hit this blunt?"

“Hell yea now that’s what I’m talking about. I didn’t know Vanessa was your cousin how are ya’ll related?”

“Her pops and my Mom is sister and brother but they haven’t spoke in years, some old family bullshit. So I don’t really know her.”

“Well, I know this about her. She’s square!”

They laugh and keep smoking and rocking to the music the perfect couple cause they both low down.

Jarvis is not saying much as he is driving around.

“Jarvis are you ok?”

"Yea, I'm sorry baby I was just thinking about showing you what the house looks like on the outside. However, we will be moving in soon. Vanessa, I want you to keep the move to yourself, it's something about Tranetta that just don't sit right with me."

"She can be a little hard to figure out. There's times when she is too moody for me."

"Yea, she seems like she can be a hand full so just keep it our business under wraps."

"Ok, I guess she may make a love connection with Odell maybe that might work for her."

"Maybe, here we are this will be your new home."

"Jarvis it's beautiful, look at the landscaping. This is a dream home I can hardly wait to see inside."

Vanessa phone is ringing with guess who? Sheka.

"It's Sheka you think I should answer?"

"Yea, answer it and tell her about herself and that I'm with you now and see what she says."

"Hello"

"Hey Nessa why haven't you called me?"

"Sheka, I haven't called you because I found out you are a low down dirty tramp. I know what happened that night; you spiked that punch so I would get drunk and you know what happened to me and lied to my face. You are not a friend to me you are nothing to me and don't ever call me again and another thing I GOT YO MAN BITCH!!" Vanessa hangs up in sheka's face.

Sheka immediately calls Jarvis and he is more than happy to receive her call this time.

"Jarvis, I just called Vanessa and she tells me you and her are together now is that true?"

"Yes it is and I am going to marry her, Sheka I want you to lose my number because it's a wrap good bye."

Sheka is furious

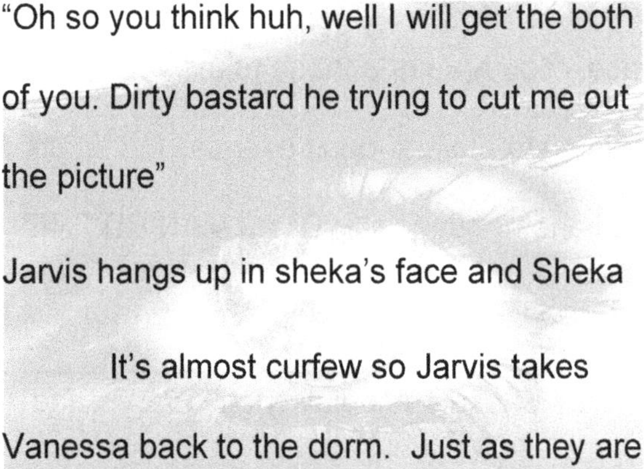

"Oh so you think huh, well I will get the both of you. Dirty bastard he trying to cut me out the picture"

Jarvis hangs up in sheka's face and Sheka

It's almost curfew so Jarvis takes Vanessa back to the dorm. Just as they are coming up Odell is leaving. They all speak and Odell keeps walking.

"Good night love I can hardly wait to be yours forever. I can't hide this ring it's so big and beautiful."

"You don't have to it's none of anyone's business.'

"Well, good night baby see you later."

Vanessa walks in and Tranetta is smiling. "I take it you and Odell hit it off."

"He's cool I don't know about hitting it off although, you and Jarvis seems to be getting quite close."

"Yea, he is a sweetheart and I really do adore him." Tranetta does not answer because she is secretly very jealous of

Vanessa and Jarvis relationship. “So Vanessa what are you doing for Thanks giving?”

“I will probably go home I’m not sure yet or I may wait until Christmas break.” “What’s your plans?”

“Not sure” Tranetta’s phone rings and its Andre.

“Hey baby can you get out?”

“No it’s pass curfew”

“Baby I really need to see you but if you can’t make it you just can’t make it.” “How about tomorrow, is that ok?’

"Maybe I guess." Andre hangs up before Tranetta can get a word in. Tranetta cusses and slams her phone shut.

"Is everything alright Tranetta."

"Yea" Tranetta walks back to her bedroom and goes to bed. Vanessa decides to stay up and figure out how she is going to tell her parents about her engagement to Jarvis. Thanksgiving holiday is just around the corner and Vanessa needs to come up with a plan soon because her belly is poking just a little but not too noticeable. Vanessa calls her mom

"Hey moms are you sleep?"

"No baby, how are you?"

"I am doing great mom, I'm in love."

"What with whom when did all this happen?"

"You remember Jarvis?"

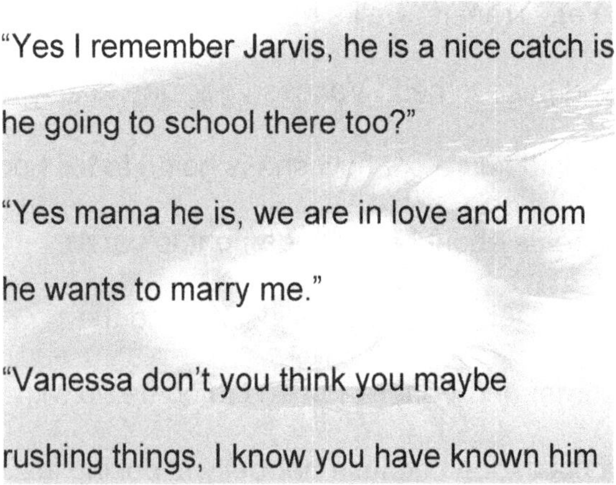

"Yes I remember Jarvis, he is a nice catch is he going to school there too?"

"Yes mama he is, we are in love and mom he wants to marry me."

"Vanessa don't you think you maybe rushing things, I know you have known him since childhood and of course he comes from a good family but at the same time dear this may be too soon. Have you thought about this, what about school, where will you live?"

"Its ok mama, Jarvis has taken care of all that he purchased us a beautiful home in River Oaks and I am still going to continue my education and so will Jarvis." "Oh Vanessa this is a lot to take in oh my God, Vanessa are you pregnant?" Vanessa is silent.

"You are Vanessa you are pregnant, I am so disappointed in you right now. Then you need to get married right away before your father finds out about this. We cannot tell him you are pregnant, are you showing?"

"Not yet just a little."

“Good come home for Thanksgiving and bring Jarvis so Jarvis can ask for your hand and please tell him not to mention the pregnancy.”

“Mama, I need you please don’t be upset with me I promise I will not drop from school.”

“Vanessa we will talk about this later right now I need to lie down and let this all soak in so I will talk to you soon love you good night.”

“Good night mama” Vanessa is feeling bad about having to lie to her mother but it is still better than telling her the truth.

Move in day for Jarvis and Vanessa

The day has come for Jarvis and Vanessa to move in together. Vanessa is thinking what a wonderful time it is and how going home for Thanksgiving is going to be exciting yet a mystery as to how her daddy is going to react to the news. Vanessa is also getting ready to break the news to Tranetta that she is moving out.

"Morning Vanessa girl I have a splitting headache this morning."

"I have some aspirin would you like some?"

"Yes please"

Vanessa walks to her room to get the aspirin when Tranetta discovers boxes by the kitchen door.

"Vanessa, what are these boxes for?"

Vanessa walks out with the aspirin and stops, feeling bad about not telling Tranetta sooner that she is moving.

"Here's the aspirin. Tranetta I should have told you sooner but, I didn't know for sure but I am moving in today with Jarvis."

Tranetta is angry and lashes out at Vanessa

"What! You could have told me Vanessa I thought we were friends! You have the nerves to just now tell me the day you are moving like I'm suppose to be good with that!"

"Hey this is really none of your dam business. It would have been nice to tell you but I'm not obligated to tell you a damned thing so you can get with that and furthermore, I don't want to do your funky ass attitude anymore!" Jarvis hears the loud voices and knocks at the door.

"Hey what's going on?"

"Nothing lets get my things and go."

"Yea get your shit and get out I don't need you as my friend anyway."

"Good then shut the hell up and keep it moving."

"Ladies calm down Tranetta its not like you will never see Vanessa again."

"Fuck you Jarvis if it wasn't for you she wouldn't be leaving so get the fuck out of my face."

"Now you fucking up Tranetta talking to my man like that don't make me get in your ass."

"You feel like you bad enough come on with it BITCH!" Jarvis gets in between them.

"Ok that's enough Vanessa get your things and lets go." Vanessa and Jarvis get the boxes and leave. Tranetta slams the door behind them.

"Fucken bitch I will make her ass pay for this."

Jarvis and Vanessa arrive at their new home and when Jarvis opens the door he hands Vanessa the keys and welcomes her home.

"Oh my God this place is more beautiful then I imagined. Jarvis I am so happy."

"I'm happy that you are happy come on let me show you the rest of your new home."

Back at Tranetta's she is still fuming when Andre calls to see if he can use her for sex again.

"Hey baby doll can you come out and play with daddy today?" Tranetta is all smiles and have seemed to forgot about Vanessa for now.

"Hey I got a great idea how about you come in the dorm nobody will see you I will come out and walk you in how about that?"

"Cool, I'm right outside, come get me girl." Tranetta rushes out the door to meet her playmate. Tranetta and Andre are back in the dorm getting hot and heavy when Odell knocks at the door.

“You expecting someone Tranetta?”

“No, cause Vanessa moved out today.”

Tranetta goes to look through the peep hole to see who it is.

“Shh, it’s nobody” Tranetta whispers to Andre “It’s just the dorm manager. Tranetta takes Andre by the hand and they creep quietly to the bedroom and finish the love session. Andre has gotten what he come for now is ready to keep moving.

“Where are you going Andre it’s still early I thought I would whip us up something to eat so you can taste how good I cook.”

"Maybe later, right now I have some business to tend to."

"Are you coming back later?"

"Probably not"

"Well when will I see you again?"

"Soon baby why you tripping Tranetta?"

"I'm not tripping its just that we hardly see one another as it is and I just want to spend time with you." Andre sits on the bed to reassure Tranetta.

"Baby its all good I'll be back I know you have curfew and I may not make it in time besides I don't want to get you in any trouble. I will call you later so we can hook up later in the week ok."

"Ok"

Andre leaves thinking to himself how he needs to chill with Tranetta because she is getting to emotional. Tranetta on the other hand is feeling like there is something going on with Andre she should know about and decides to go back to his place before her curfew. Tranetta gets dressed and goes to Andre's house. Andre's son comes to the door.

"Who is it?"

"I'm looking for Andre."

"Mommy a woman is here looking for daddy?" when Tranetta hears that she almost passes out. Andre wife comes to the door drying her hands from doing the dishes.

"May I help you?"

Tranetta thinks of a quick lie.

"Yes, I'm Tranetta Baker with the University, I'm a student and we are in the neighborhood doing surveys on African-American fathers and husbands who are still displaying positive leadership for their families." Tranetta quickly whips out her student badge.

"Well my husband is not home right now if there is anything I can help you with I will be happy to assist you."

"Great just a few questions and I'll let you back to your house work."

"Come in I can give you about ten minutes then I need to go."

"Ok that's more then enough time."

Tranetta walks in and have a seat in the living room and takes out a pen and pad.

"First question, what is your husband last name?"

"Crawford"

"How long have you been married"

"We have been married for ten years."

"How many children do you have?"

"We have two beautiful children."

"Would you say your husband is a good role model for the family?"

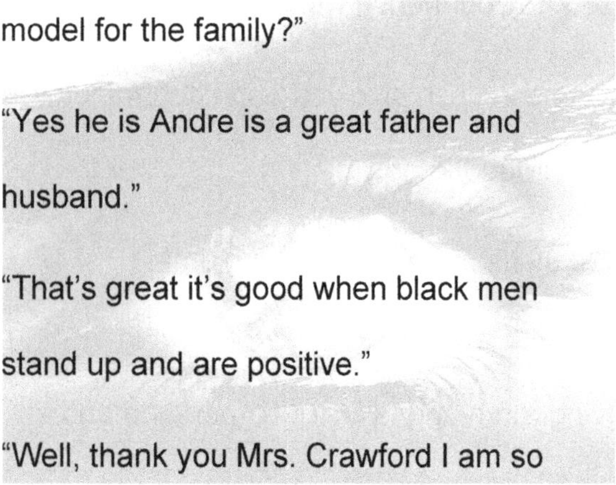

"Yes he is Andre is a great father and husband."

"That's great it's good when black men stand up and are positive."

"Well, thank you Mrs. Crawford I am so sorry I didn't get your first name."

"Oh I'm Debra I hope I was able to help you and I think this is a good survey. My husband is one of many black men that is a good father and husband. That's my baby."

"Wonderful well Debra it was good talking with you."

"Ok have a good day."

"You too bye."

Tranetta is so mad she is walking like she is on fire.

"That BASTARD why he trying to play me, that's cool because little do you know Mr. Andre Crawford you just stepped in some shit." Tranetta calls Andre

"What up girl?"

"You tell me"

"What you talking about girl?"

"You are a liar I met your little family MOTHERFUCKER!"

"What"

"Yea I went by your house, don't worry your precious little wife don't know anything I played it off."

"Why the FUCK you go your ass over my house for?"

"I needed to know who the woman and kids really were now I know."

"Bitch you tripping lose my fucken number hoe." Andre Hangs up in Tranetta's face.

"I know he didn't."

Tranetta calls back and gets no answer from Andre now she is hotter than fish grease. Tranetta has never had any success at love, just when she thought she could trust again she now has to step back into her ways of the streets.

"Tranetta wait up"

Odell walking fast trying to catch up to Tranetta but she is so mad she pays no attention. Odell finally catches up to her and Tranetta turns around to him.

"Girl you walking like you trying to get to some free chicken or something."

"Ha ha you're so funny I really forgot to laugh."

"What's up with you? Did I do something to upset you?"

Tranetta loosens up a bit

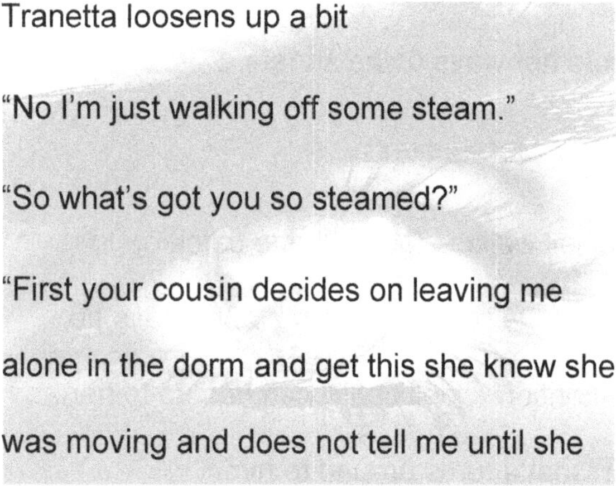

"No I'm just walking off some steam."

"So what's got you so steamed?"

"First your cousin decides on leaving me alone in the dorm and get this she knew she was moving and does not tell me until she packed and ready to go this morning."

"Yea that is kind of messed up but, forget that girl she may be my cousin but she stuck up as hell we not that close her family think they are better than the rest you know what I'm saying?"

"You right she does act like she the queen of shit."

"So let her go she better off where she is anyway."

"You know she moved in with ya boy Jarvis and check this out the bitch is pregnant."

Odell world starts to spin on that

"Say listen let me get back to you later I need to run to my room, is it ok if I stop through later?"

"As long as it's before curfew."

"I know I'll be back"

Tranetta gets back to her dorm and fix something to eat and wait on Odell to come by.

One month later Thanksgiving Holiday

"Jarvis hurry up we need to get to the airport before we miss our flight." "Here I come I'm just making sure we haven't left anything."

Jarvis runs down the stairs and hugs Vanessa from behind.

"I love you so much Vanessa, you know it's a good thing you are barely showing. I know you told your mom but it's your dad I'm worried about. Speaking of that I thought it would be nice to get married Christmas that way you will only be slightly poking out. This will also be good for the baby to be born into wedlock."

"You know what, I can get with that. I am nervous about your parents as well."

"No problem mom and dad think the world of you always has and besides they want a grand baby. However, they think we should get married right away." Jarvis and Vanessa head to the airport.

Jarvis pulls into the driveway of Vanessa's parents and is greeted by Tiffany.

"Hey Vanessa I missed you so much let me look at you."

"Tiffany man you are growing like a weed girl."

Tiffany takes Vanessa by the hand and walk into the house.

"Look mom and Dad guess who I found wondering around lost."

"Vanessa, oh my baby Terry isn't she absolutely beautiful?' Terry is not as eager as everyone else because he is disappointed to find out Vanessa and Jarvis is engaged but he still does not know about the baby. Terry is looking Jarvis up and down

"How you doing Jarvis come let's talk ladies, if you would excuse us." Jarvis and Terry go into the family room for privacy. Vanessa, her mother and Tiffany go into the kitchen.

"Jarvis please have a seat son. Jarvis I understand you and Vanessa are engaged."

"Yes sir I love Vanessa always have since we were kids."

"I see well, Jarvis you know how I feel about my daughter; she is very precious to me and her mother. Kathy is excited and I'm sure Vanessa is as well. But I'm not so sure about all this. I know you are financially stable and you come from a good family however, do you really want to get married?"

"Yes sir, I am ready to spend the rest of my life with Vanessa I promise I will be good to her and take care of her."

Terry just sits staring at Jarvis for about a good minute.

"Ok I'm going to hold you to that but remember this as long as my daughter is happy we are happy too but if you make her un happy then you will have to answer to me."

"I understand and I won't let her or you down."

"Good deal then you have my blessings welcome to the family."

Jarvis is thinking how glad he is that part of the visit is out of the way.

"Come on son let's go see what the ladies are up to."

Jarvis and Terry walk into the kitchen. Terry gives Vanessa a big hug and kiss. Kathy is so excited to have her daughter home.

"We need to talk sleeping arrangements."

"Oh no Mrs. Kathy I will be at my parents and visit you all."

“Oh yea I forgot your parents live here well then it’s settled. I have a great idea how about you and your parents join us for Thanks giving Dinner.”

“That’s very kind of you I will tell them and see what they say.” Jarvis gives Vanessa a hug before leaving to see his parents.

“Hey mom”

“Jarvis is here” screams his mom Tonya. Jarvis father comes into the living room. “Son, good to see you, where is Vanessa?”

“She is at her parents getting some rest I’ll get her later and bring her back to see you.”

"Are you hungry Jarvis cause mama made your favorite meal, Seafood Gumbo and Peach cobbler"

"Well in that case lead me to the kitchen so I can get my eat on."

They all go into the dining room for a hearty meal.

"Son what happened to that crazy girl you were dating?"

"Sheka"

"Yea her"

"I had to get rid of her she is not for me."

"Ooh, I am so happy to hear that. Sheka was about to make me step off in her ass."

"Mom"

"Well it's the truth that girl is rude and thinks she owns the world."

"Ok moving forward Mom, Dad Vanessa's parents would like us to come for Thanksgiving Dinner this Thursday that is if you don't have plans."

"Jarvis you know we always have company over for the Holidays. Your Aunt Willa and her family, your Grand Mother and some other folk we don't know that tag along with them I have planned a big feast and I know you better bring Vanessa for dessert at least."

"Please forgive me, I lost my head for a moment, I guess this is going to be a big feast for me, you know I have to show up at Vanessa's parents but I promise mom I won't eat too much." Jarvis phone rings and its sheka, but Jarvis ignores her call.

Sheka is in revenge mode, she happens to be home as well.

"If they think they are going to get away with this they got another thing coming." Sheka then calls Vanessa.

"What do you want Sheka?"

"Bitch you got me messed up if you think you are going to steal Jarvis from me." "No you got yourself messed up Heifer cause he is my man so live with it and move on Sheka game over BITCH!"

Vanessa hangs up in sheka's face. This makes her even more steamed. Sheka is holding the phone with malice in her heart.

"I hate that trick that's why I jacked her drink up, now I'm gonna have to get that ass."

Jarvis calls Vanessa to check on her.

"Jarvis sheka is tripping she had the nerve to call me and actually think you still want her."

"She called me too but I didn't answer, just don't answer her anymore, she will get tired and stop."

"I don't know J she seem like she is obsessed or something."

"Don't worry about her, on a good note would you like to go to the movies tonight and lets take Tiff with us."

"Sounds like a date to me I'll let Tiff know she would like that. Thanks for considering her."

"Of course just call me Mr. Considerate."

"Ok Mr. considerate what time should we be ready?"

"I thought we would catch the nine o'clock so about eight."

"We'll be ready, see you then." Vanessa goes downstairs to let Tiff know she has been invited to the movies.

"Hey Tiffy where are you?"

"In the kitchen sis"

"Jarvis wants to know if you want to go to the movies with us tonight."

"Yes, yes, yes what time are we leaving?"

"Be ready for eight"

Tiffy drops everything and run upstairs to get ready.

"Thanks for allowing me to hang out with you guys J it was a lot of fun but I must get my beauty rest so good night Vanessa, good night J."

"Good night Tiff see you in the morning and don't forget Mom wants us to help her with dinner early so be ready."

"I will adios."

Tiffy goes upstairs to leave Jarvis and Vanessa some private time.

"Jarvis you know sometimes I wonder if I should have called the police and made a report about you know what happened to me."

“You don’t know what really happened so what would you have told them?”

“I don’t know this is all still crazy to me and sometime I wake up shaking, I am still very afraid.” Jarvis hold Vanessa close to him.

“It’s going to be alright Vanessa just trust me. I promise to take care of you, I just want you to put all this out of your mind and allow me to love the pain away.” “You are a wonderful man Jarvis what would I do without you.” Vanessa lays her head into Jarvis chest.

“Come here sit down Vanessa, I want to get married Christmas Day.”

"Christmas, are you sure?"

"Yes I'm very sure I have never been sure of anything in my life."

"There is so much to do first we have to tell our parents and figure out where we want to do this."

"Whatever you want is what we will do, so it's all good right."

"Yes, oh Jarvis you have made me the happiest woman in the world."

"I need to get out of here so I will see you tomorrow for dinner oh and please give your parents my parents regrets we have a load of relatives coming in some of them are probably at the house already."

"I'll tell them now give me some of those juicy lips before you go." Jarvis plants a long hot kiss on Vanessa and leaves.

Thanksgiving Day

Jarvis parent's house is filled with the scents of delicious foods and relatives. Jarvis is awaken by his cousin Yolanda little two year old son whose throwing a ball over Jarvis head and hitting the wall over the head board.

"Hey what are you doing? Go play with that ball outside." Screams Jarvis.

"Oh there you are I'm sorry J he knows better I guess he decided to wake you up but I'm thinking that was not a good idea Jamal."

"You're right Jamal that's not cool man." Jamal runs out of the room and downstairs.

"I'm out of here I'll see you down stairs cuz Aunt Tonya is hooking it up."

Jarvis gets out of bed and shower thinking about his love Vanessa when his phone rings and its Sheka again.

"This girl is bugging, now she stalking I'm gonna change my number." Jarvis just ignores her call and continue dressing.

Jarvis comes downstairs says hello and gives hugs to everyone and heads for the door.

"Mr. Jarvis" calls Tonya "Where are you going so early?"

"I'm going to Vanessa's and then we are going to come back here remember I told you yesterday?"

"Don't be too late dinner is at four."

"We will be here love you mama."

Terry answers the door with a smile and a cigar.

"Hello Mr. Jarvis, how's it going son?"

"Very well thank you for asking." Terry calls for Vanessa to come down. Vanessa walks into the den and sees Jarvis and breaks out with a big smile.

"Well I'll leave you two alone I need to go to the store for your Mother this will be a all day affair."

"Hey baby, you look beautiful this morning."

"I don't feel so beautiful I have been sick all night."

"What's wrong?"

"I have been just nauseated feeling like I want to throw up but nothing is coming up."

"Soon as we get back home you are going to the doctor but right now I can get you some ginger ale that should settle your stomach."

"You don't have to leave we have some in the fridge I didn't think about that." Vanessa goes to get a glass of ginger ale. Kathy is in the kitchen mixing and blending.

"Vanessa dear are you ok? You look kind of pale."

"Just a little nauseated."

"There's some ginger ale in the fridge. Make sure you drink it cold. Did I hear Jarvis in the den?"

"Yea he's watching the game do you need me to help you?"

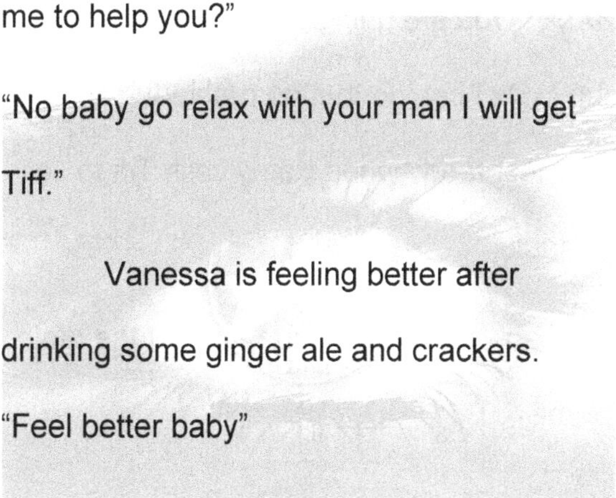

"No baby go relax with your man I will get Tiff."

Vanessa is feeling better after drinking some ginger ale and crackers.

"Feel better baby"

"Yes" Vanessa thanking Jarvis, you are so sweet to me."

"When are we going to tell our parents about our wedding plans?"

"I'm thinking since you are the man, and you came up with the idea, you can break the news to my parents at dinner then yours at your parent's house."

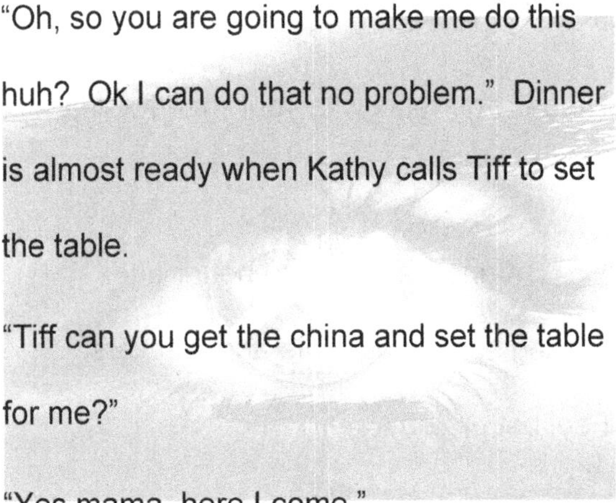

"Oh, so you are going to make me do this huh? Ok I can do that no problem." Dinner is almost ready when Kathy calls Tiff to set the table.

"Tiff can you get the china and set the table for me?"

"Yes mama, here I come."

Terry is ready to get the turkey carved and eat so he can get back to his game. The table is set with beautiful linens, china, candles and an array of delicious foods. Terry blesses the food and carves the turkey.

"Thank you for inviting me to share dinner with you all everything look so delicious."

"You are always welcome Jarvis enjoy your meal." Jarvis is feeling nervous about breaking the news but decides to speak up anyway.

"May I have everyone's attention please? I can't think of a better occasion to announce that Vanessa and me are planning to marry on Christmas day and would love to have our wedding here in our home town."

Tiffany eyes light up, Kathy is smiling so big and terry is surprised.

Kathy speaks out of joy "I think that's a wonderful idea, we can start plans today Vanessa."

"Works for me mom, where are we starting first?"

"I was thinking we can start with the colors then work our way through. By the time you leave child we will have everything in place and all ya'll have to do is show up."

"You are the best Mother a girl can ask for thanks Mom. Jarvis let's get to your parents before they think we have forgotten about

them."

"Yea I don't want to get hit with a frying pan, it was a pleasure everything was A+.

Jarvis and Vanessa are at Jarvis parent's house ready to share in the festivities.

"What took you two so long?"

"Sorry Mom Vanessa Mother put together a feast out of this world."

"I hope you have room for your Mother's Dressing."

"Yes Mother I have room for everything bring it on."

Vanessa is looking at the sweet potato pie as though she wants to tear into it without a fork. “Vanessa sit have whatever you want love.” “I think I will start with some of that sweet potato pie I could smell it outside.” Everyone is settling down when Jarvis makes the announcement that he and Vanessa will marry Christmas Day. “That is wonderful.” Jarvis Mother and everyone are excited at the news. “Will the wedding be here Vanessa?” “Yes Mam, my mom and I are going to start working on the plans tomorrow.” “Beautiful, if you guys need some help please let me know.” Jarvis is sitting back in his chair barely able to move from two delicious Thanksgiving meals. "I am stuffed." Jarvis holding his stomach. "Vanessa can you help me up?" Vanessa laughs "Are you kidding, who's going to help me?" Jarvis finally makes it up and thanks his parents for a lovely dinner.

"I better get you back to your parents Vanessa before they think I've kidnapped you."

"Ha, ha you are too funny, thanks for dinner, I had a good time."

"You are so welcome Vanessa, and don't forget if you and your mom need some help with the wedding plans please, don't hesitate to call me."

Jarvis and Vanessa returns home as they approach their front door Vanessa discovers a note with her name on it. Vanessa quickly puts the note into her purse without Jarvis seeing it because he was busy in the trunk taking out their luggage. Vanessa walks upstairs and goes into the bathroom and takes the note out. To Vanessa's surprise the note does not have a name of which it's from just the words "I know who your baby's father is slut." Vanessa is terrified and confused, she has no idea who could have left the note because no one knows where she and

Jarvis lives. Jarvis calls Vanessa from the bottom of the stairs. "Vanessa, are you ok up there?"

"Yes baby I'm good, I'll be down in a minute ok." Vanessa tears the note up and flushes it down the toilet and goes downstairs.

"Well, there's my sweet wife to be is you ok baby you look a little sad?"

"I'm fine just a little tired from the trip and hungry."

"No problem you sit right here and put your feet up and let daddy handle dinner arrangements."

Jarvis goes into the kitchen and returns with a handful of delivery menus.

“Which one do you prefer my queen?”

“Let’s see how about some Dominoes pizza?”

“Good choice I’ll call them right up so is the meat lover’s good?”

“Perfect and get some wings too.”

“Finally the pizza is here I thought they would never get here.”

“It’s only been twenty minutes; I guess the baby is hungry huh.” Jarvis gets money and pay for the pizza. They eat, watch movies and go to bed.

"Good morning J do you have a busy day?"

"Yes, I have classes then the meeting for the business I am starting."

"Really, you didn't tell me about this."

"It was supposed to be a surprise but since you know now I am going to be opening a new coffee café and book store with wireless access. What you think?" "I think that's great."

"So are you busy today besides going to class."

"No just class then some grocery shopping then home to wait on my man." Jarvis and Vanessa kiss at their cars and leave.

"Look who decides to come to school." Tranetta is being sarcastic towards Vanessa.

"Listen Tranetta I don't want to fight with you, I really want to be friends with you."

"You can save that drama for your mama lil girl cause I don't want to be friends with you."

"Fine, then if you would excuse me I have better things to do besides being in the company of a miserable bitch."

"Did you just call me a bitch?" Vanessa just walks pass Tranetta and goes to class.

Vanessa can't seem to concentrate for thinking about the note she got when she arrived home yesterday. Vanessa is now five months pregnant and still does not know who fathered her baby. Although, she's happy with Jarvis she still gets side tracked wondering why he is being so nice to her when he can be with someone with less drama. Odell sees Vanessa as she is leaving class but she doesn't see him Odell notice that Vanessa is pregnant. Odell begins to feel sick from the thought that his cousin could be pregnant by one of his friends. Odell immediately goes to transfer and leaves school without telling anyone. "Dam Tranetta is not lying about Vanessa being pregnant. I better get out of this school before Vanessa finds out what happened." Odell whispering to himself as sweat is beading on his forehead. As Odell is leaving to get into his car Tranetta calls out to him.

"Hey Odell where are you going?"

"I have an emergency at home with my Mom so I am leaving to go back home."

"So you were just going to leave without saying goodbye?"

"Well I am in kind of a hurry. Listen, Tranetta I am not the one I wish you success in your quest here. I have to leave so now goodbye is that good enough for you?"

"Wow, you are a piece of work Odell, but it's all good go on get out of my face punk ass lil boy." Tranetta storms away cussing as she is quickly walking away from Odell. Odell just waves his hand and gets in his car and leave. Tranetta's cell phone rings and its Andre.

"Hey Tranetta can I see you tonight?"

"Maybe"

"Oh so you mad at me listen Tranetta I should have told you about my wife but, I didn't want to get you involved with our mess, I'm not happy with her its you I want baby just give me a little time and she will be out the picture I'm divorcing her"

"If that is what you want and yes, I am mad at you."

"Come on baby, I will make it up to you."

"I'm sure and just as we get a good night going I'm sure you will get an emergency call."

"I promise my phone will be off so I can concentrate on you and only you."

"Well in that case I can see you. What time should I be ready?"

"How about eight o'clock is that good for you?"

"Can we make it earlier about six thirty you know I have curfew."

"Ok I will see you then."

"Ok bye sweetie"

Back at Vanessa and Jarvis home Vanessa is upset about the note and wants to call the police but is too afraid. Vanessa just try to put this out of her mind when Jarvis walks in.

"Jarvis you are finally home come here baby and give me a hug." Jarvis gives Vanessa a big hug and notice that she is shaking.

"What's wrong baby you are shaking is everything alright? Did something happen?"

"No I'm just happy you are home. Are you hungry I grilled some steaks."

"Yes I am it smells delicious."

Vanessa phone rings with an unknown number. When she answers the caller hangs up.

"Baby, who was that on the phone?"

"Wrong number" Vanessa is concerned now that someone is trying to torment her.

"Vanessa, it's almost Christmas and you know what that means, you will be my beautiful wife."

"Just the thought of us getting married is blowing me away."

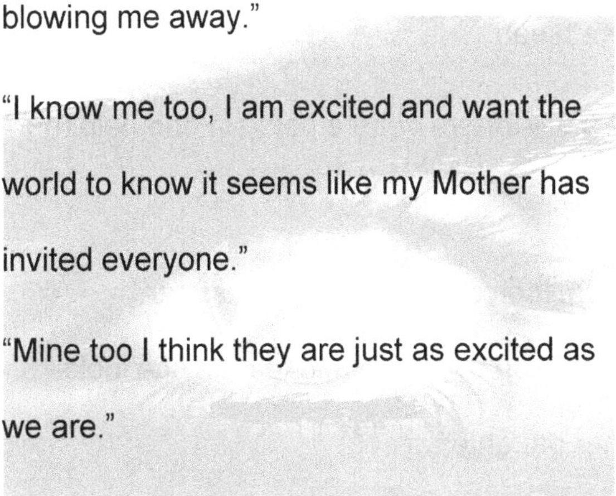

"I know me too, I am excited and want the world to know it seems like my Mother has invited everyone."

"Mine too I think they are just as excited as we are."

"I booked our flight and we should be there three days before the wedding." "Cool that gives me time to get the final touches together."

Christmas Day Jarvis and Vanessa's Wedding

"Vanessa are you in there?" calls Kathleen

"Yes Mother I'm here come in and help me please."

"Oh, look at my beautiful daughter." Kathleen eyes begin to tear as she looks her daughter over.

"Momma I am so nervous, I feel like I'm about to throw up."

"Calm down baby it's going to be alright, take a deep breath, here drink some water."

"Thanks Momma, were you nervous when you and Daddy got married?"

"Oh my God I was terrified to say the least when those Chapel doors opened I almost ran away but, then I saw your Father's handsome face and all my fears just went away." Kathleen helps Vanessa to finish getting dressed; Vanessa is beautiful in a Vera Wang wedding gown fit for a grand occasion. Vanessa is carrying her pregnancy well you can hardly see she is pregnant. Sheka is disguised among the many guest, fuming from hurt feeling betrayed by Jarvis & Vanessa. Sheka got her information from the community paper cause nobody invited her.

"I can't believe this tramp! Plus she has the nerves to be pregnant, well let's just see what happens when I put the ruins on their little happy future." Sheka is whispering to herself and grinning with a little devious smirk.

Later at the reception Jarvis goes to the restroom with Sheka close behind. Jarvis goes into the stall when his door suddenly opens and to his surprise its Sheka.

"Sheka, what the hell are you doing here?"

"You dirty rotten dog I should have known you two were having an affair. Is she why you dumped me? After she slutted around you have the nerves to marry her, oh, and let's not mention she is pregnant. How can you do me this way Jarvis?" Sheka begins to cry. I think you have plans to cut me out for good, well, we will see."

"Are you insane? You know we were through a long time ago, now get out of here before I have security throw you out!" Jarvis walks pass Sheka leaving her to feel sorry for herself. Sheka discreetly leaves but vows to herself that no man will ever hurt her this way again.

Back at the campus Tranetta has been stood up by Andre once again. "That's it I'm done with his ass I can't keep letting him get away with this." Tranetta goes to Andre's house to let him know she will not be sloppy seconds. Tranetta gets to the house to find it empty Andre and his family is gone. Tranetta calls Andre's phone but, his number has been changed. Lonely, heartbroken and angry Tranetta walks back to the dorm totally disappointed in the love she thought she finally had. Back at the dorm Tranetta cries herself to sleep.

"Jarvis I am so happy to finally be your wife, ooh, that has a nice ring to it."

"Yes it does and I can't wait to give you everything you deserve." The happy couple snuggles together in marital bliss with smiles on their faces.

One month later

Jarvis is in the bathroom on his cell phone whispering when Vanessa awakens. "Jarvis, are you in the bathroom honey." "Yes, just a minute." Jarvis tells his caller he has to go and hangs up. Jarvis comes out of the bathroom and walks pass Vanessa as though he has an attitude. "Jarvis, baby what's wrong?"

"Nothing I thought you had to use the bathroom." Vanessa just turns and goes into the bathroom with a concerned look on her face. When she comes out Jarvis has already left. Vanessa calls Jarvis but he does not answer her call.

"I wonder what his problem is." Vanessa shrugs it off and gets ready to go to class. Jarvis is beginning to show his true colors, not the man Vanessa and everyone else thinks he is. Back at the house Vanessa is making dinner when Jarvis walks in with an attitude.

"Hey baby are you hungry because I have a sweet surprise for you." Vanessa is feeling loving with happiness in her voice. Jarvis just looks at her and walks right pass her not saying anything hangs his suit jacket and proceed upstairs. Vanessa right behind her husband wants to know what's wrong. "Jarvis are you ok honey?"

Jarvis gets to the top of the stairs and turns to Vanessa looking angry. "Why are you following me Vanessa, can I come into my home without you sweating me?" Vanessa is surprised at the way Jarvis is acting and decides to go back downstairs. Jarvis goes into the bedroom closes the door and makes a phone call. Vanessa is feeling hurt and confused by Jarvis sudden attitude towards her. Jarvis makes a call to a mystery person when he is done Jarvis just runs down the stairs and leaves slamming the door behind him. Vanessa goes to the window and watch Jarvis pull out of the driveway with tears in her eyes, feeling confused and hurt. Vanessa slowly sits down from cramps she feels in her lower abdomen. "Oh, I need to lay down" Vanessa talking to herself turns to put her feet up and lay on the sofa in hopes that the cramps will ease, however, the pain continues, getting harder for her to bear. Vanessa reaches for her phone and calls Jarvis but gets his voicemail. Tears running down her face Vanessa gather her strength gets off the sofa, grabs her car keys and drives herself to the hospital. Once Vanessa arrives at the hospital as she walks through the automatic doors everything starts to spin and Vanessa collapse. Medical personnel immediately respond to Vanessa getting her into a room. Vanessa is unconscious, blood pressure elevated; pulse pounding the doctor makes the call to rush Vanessa immediately to icu to monitor her. In the meantime Jarvis is having a hot time with Tranetta. Jarvis and Tranetta have been secretly seeing one another while Tranetta is still trying to find the where bouts of Andre who has slipped out of existence. Jarvis bids Tranetta good bye after a wild ride of lust and betrayal.

"Jarvis, what are we going to do about Vanessa?"

"You let me handle Vanessa, don't worry your pretty little head I got that all wrapped. You just keep it warm while I go play the honorable hubby."

Jarvis goes into the house to find Vanessa gone. Jarvis realizes he turned his ringer off and checks his phone to find a number called from the hospital and calls back. "Yes this is Jarvis someone called me from this number." The nurse on the other end confirms that Vanessa is in icu and that he needs to come to the hospital. Jarvis quickly arrives to icu and see Vanessa lying helplessly with tubes and monitors. The Doctor walks in

"Are you her husband?"

"Yes sir is my wife going to be alright, what happened?" The doctor looks at Jarvis with concern.

"Well, your wife seems to have slipped into a coma from what I have diagnosed her as having Toxemia." Jarvis head in a whirlwind.

"Toxemia what the hell is that?"

"It's when a woman has a build up of toxic sodium in the blood and urine causing her to have an elevated or dramatic drop in blood pressure in your wife case she had a significant elevated pressure causing her to go into a coma, now this can be temporary. We will monitor and see in a few days if we need to deliver the baby by cesarean and of course the baby is fine but we want to monitor and see how the baby is getting along if at anytime the baby gets into trouble we will deliver the baby immediately."

Jarvis is stunned, but nevertheless is still contemplating his plans for Vanessa. Jarvis has been playing her all along. Jarvis calls Vanessa's parents to let them know what has happened, they rush to Texas to be with their daughter. Jarvis sits with Vanessa and comfort her in front of the staff as they are checking blood pressure and monitors but as soon as they leave Jarvis bends over Vanessa with shocking words. "Vanessa I want you to die. I need to inherit the rewards, so go BITCH!" Vanessa can hear Jarvis she just can't respond trapped in fear her mind is reeling as she fights to come back but just can't seem to make the connection to awaken. The next day Vanessa's parents has arrived and Kathleen is devastated at the sight of her daughter laying in a coma.

“Jarvis what happened to my baby?” Kathleen is crying. Terry is holding Vanessa hand and whispering loving words to her to come back. Jarvis starts to tell them what the doctor said when Dr. Ross walks into the room.

“Hello I’m Dr. Ross”

“Hello I’m Vanessa mother Kathleen and this is her father Terry doctor please tell us what’s going on with our daughter.” Jarvis phone is vibrating its Sheka. The doctor is talking to Vanessa’s parents Jarvis excuses himself to take Sheka's call "What's up Sheka, what do you want?"

"I need to talk to you."

"Not now I have something important going on."

"You mean like your little darling wife sleeping or should I say hanging on by a thread yea nigga I know what's up, you been playing the shit out of her. I know all about the money, the will, the inheritance at first I was stomped as to why you just all of a sudden went that direction but now I know everything."

"What, girl you are tripping?"

"Whatever player you can't get shit passed me remember, you can't slick a can of oil. Now, I want in or I am going to blow your cover you got 24 hours to hook me up with the outcome or I'm going to blow the whistle." Sheka hangs up in Jarvis face and smiles at her self in the mirror with a sneaky evil look. Jarvis is feeling pressured and wondering how Sheka could have possibly found out what he up to. Jarvis goes back into the room and tells Vanessa's parents he needs to go freshen up. Kathleen hugs Jarvis.

"Thank you for calling us right away Jarvis. Go freshen up and get you some rest you must be tired." Jarvis is walking and turns around

"Oh, forgive me for being rude do you need to stay at the house I can take your things with me."

"Well, we can get our things thank you for the offer and we will come to the house later sweetie ok."

"Ok Mom love you, I will be back in a few hours."

Jarvis goes straight to Tranetta's to fill her in on Vanessa's condition and Sheka's intentions.

"WHAT THE HELL YOU MEAN SHEKA WANTS A CUT?" screams Tranetta. "Calm down she's just bluffing."

"No we need to take care of that bitch right away where is she? Get me all her info and I will take it from there."

"What are you going to do Tranetta?"

Tranetta feeling anxious

"JUST GET ME THE DAM INFO JARVIS!" screams Tranetta.

"Ok but you got to do this clean you hear me."

"Yea I got you just leave it to me no one will ever know." Tranetta gently kisses Jarvis with an evil smirk. Jarvis gives Traneta Sheka's info and leave. Tranetta immediately puts her plans into action to shut Sheka's mouth so her and Jarvis plans are not interrupted. Jarvis is driving home nervous about Tranetta and what she is doing. Jarvis calls Vanessa's mother to check in on Vanessa's condition and to let her know he will be there soon. In the meantime Jarvis goes back to the house and start looking through Vanessa's things why? you say, because Vanessa has just inherited 30 million dollars when her very rich grandmother past two years ago and Jarvis knew about it only Vanessa does not know Jarvis knows and if she has a son the child will receive 4 million at age 18 now how's that for getting a girl to love you. Although, Jarvis and family has wealth his greed has taken him to a whole new level. However, Sheka just happen to be in the right place at the right time and found out about Jarvis intentions. So, if Vanessa dies, you got it Jarvis gets it all. Jarvis has found the deposit into Vanessa's account and the papers that states her inheritance. Jarvis is all smiles as he puts everything back in Vanessa's secret place he heads to the hospital.

Jarvis arrives to the hospital as though he is weary and concerned.

“Hey mama” Jarvis gives Kathleen a hug.

“How is my angel dong?”

“She’s still the same; all we can do is pray and wait.”

“I know you both must be exhausted, how about you go get some rest and I will stay with my wife.” Terry is firm about staying with his daughter. “No I am not leaving her.” Terry’s eyes begin to water. Kathleen consoles her husband. “I think we will be ok son we really don’t want to leave until we know something.” “Ok, just want you to be know Vanessa and the baby will be alright.”

But really Jarvis wants them to leave.

Jarvis leaves out to call Tranetta.

"Hey I'm at the hospital, what are your plans for Sheka because time is ticking."

"I know I scheduled a flight to pay her a little visit in Atlanta, she won't know what hit her."

"I hope you know what you're doing we don't need anything to go wrong."

"Don't worry about me you just handle your business with the wifey." They hang up and Tranetta goes to catch her flight.

Jarvis goes back to be with Vanessa as he gets close to her room he hears Kathleen crying he rushes in to find the doctor's and nurses all around her. "What's happening with my wife?" Kathleen is overjoyed and so is Terry.

"She woke up Jarvis the lord answered our prayers our baby is woke." Kathleen hugs and squeeze Jarvis from excitement. The doctor turns to them with a big smile. "She is doing good everything seems to be normal however, I do want to keep her for a few more nights to make sure. The baby is fine and she still has about 4 weeks to go, so she will have to take it easy. I will be back to check on her." Jarvis is playing it off well. "Thank you doctor for all your help, thank God my wife and baby is going to be ok." Jarvis calls his parents to let them know Vanessa is ok. In the meantime Tranetta has made it to Sheka's to take care of her. Sheka is walking into her apartment and is greeted by Tranetta.

"Who the hell are you and what are you doing in my apartment?" Tranetta takes another sip of wine she has helped herself to from Sheka's wine rack.

"Well, Ms. Sheka I know who you are and it has come to my attention that you have a big mouth, throwing around threats to Jarvis. Oh yea I'm Tranetta just thought I would let you know that."

“I don’t give a dam who you are get your ass out of my house.”

“Not so fast little girl, I need you to understand that you are not in power here and that your little threats are to stop now!”

“You go to hell and you can go back and tell Jarvis I am not backing off I am the one who helped him get this all together and if he thinks he is going to cut me out because he fucking you now he better think again.”

“Give it up Sheka there is no room for you anymore we got this so you keep your little mouth shut and everything will be ok for you.”

"Oh really and what is that suppose to mean?" Tranetta gets up and walks over to Sheka and looks her directly in her eyes with an evil nasty look.

"You heard me BITCH I said keep your mouth shut!" Sheka pulls out her cellphone. "Well we will see about that!" Sheka starts to dial 911 when Tranetta knocks the phone out of Sheka's hand and knocks her to the floor.

Sheka gets up and hits Tranetta back and the fight is on Sheka is whooping on Tranetta, gets her down and is on top of her choking her when Tranetta reaches in her pocket and pulls out a switch blade and cuts Sheka across the face. Sheka falls off Tranetta and rolls over holding her face. Tranetta runs into Sheka's kitchen pulls out a butcher knife, comes back to Sheka who is trying to regain herself but Tranetta start stabbing Sheka repeatedly until she falls dead. Tranetta immediately cleans the knife and puts it into her bag looks around and start cleaning her fingerprints off everything she touched, gets Sheka's cell phone, cleans herself up, changes her blood stained clothes and leaves Sheka to be found.

Tranetta calls Jarvis and tell him what happened. "Listen Jarvis I had to do it the bitch was about to call the police. I wasn't trying to kill her but she left me no other choice."

"Oh my God, just get back here as soon as you can did you clean up your mess?"

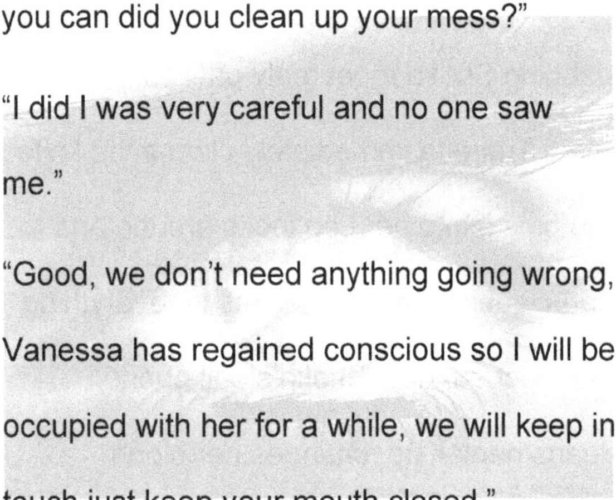

"I did I was very careful and no one saw me."

"Good, we don't need anything going wrong, Vanessa has regained conscious so I will be occupied with her for a while, we will keep in touch just keep your mouth closed."

"Ok when will I see you again?"

"Soon, just sit tight and carry on as usual soon we will have the money we need." Did you find Andre?"

"No but I could care less I don't need him anymore now that I have you."

"Cool you just remember that; I will talk to you later." Jarvis hangs up and goes back to be with Vanessa.

"Hey wifey are you ok?" Vanessa looks at Jarvis with fear in her eyes because she now knows what he is up to. Vanessa's mother takes Vanessa by the hand and kisses it and tells her she loves her.

“Vanessa, your father and I have to leave but we will be in contact constantly ok baby and when the baby is born we will be back.” Vanessa nods he head in agreement. Kathy and Terry say good bye and leave. Jarvis is relieved because now he doesn’t have to deal with Vanessa’s parents snooping around.

“Baby just relax and let me take care of you, the doctor says you will be fine and can go home in a few days.” Vanessa is terrified, thinking to herself how a man could so good be so evil. However, Vanessa plays along not letting Jarvis know that she heard every word he said to her when she was un conscious. "Baby are you comfortable, do you want something to drink, I know you must be tired from all this excitement?" Just as Jarvis is about to get Vanessa a cup of water the nurse walks in with a tray of food for Vanessa.

"Here we go Vanessa this should make you feel much better, it will take a couple of hours for you to speak because of the tube we had in your throat so I know it may feel a little sore so for now you can only have a soft diet but everything should be better by tomorrow and then the doctor can tell you if you will be able to go home ok sweetie?" Vanessa nods her head.

“Vanessa sweetheart do you need me to help you?” Vanessa shakes her head no to Jarvis.

“Well, baby its getting late I would stay but, I need to work on the proposal for the business and I also have some research to do for class but I promise you I will be here bright and early in the morning ok baby?” Vanessa shakes her head for yes; Jarvis gives Vanessa a kiss on the forehead and walk out.

Jarvis is nervous but at the same time somewhat relieved that Sheka is no longer a problem. Jarvis arrives homes to calculate his next move, hoping to get everything in order for his plan of action to take effect. "I got to keep Vanessa in the dark just a little while longer, I can't afford any slip ups or I am done for." Vanessa is in tears hardly able to believe what she has heard Jarvis say to her. As the night continues on Vanessa is exhausted and decides to handle this as it comes to her by just playing along to see where this all ends.

Jarvis is up early so he can go visit with Vanessa as he is getting out of the shower his phone rings.

"Hello"

"Jarvis it's your Mother baby I have some terrible news. Are you sitting down?" "No

Mom I just got out of the shower I am on my way to see Vanessa."

"Oh love I am sorry how is Vanessa?"

"She is going to be just fine her and the baby. Now what's wrong Mom?"

"Jarvis, Sheka was found murdered." Jarvis Mom begins to cry.

"Oh my God do they know what happened?"

"No I spoke to Sheka's parents earlier and they are on there way to her apartment. What a terrible tragedy, someone stabbed that poor child to death." "Mom, I don't know what to say, did they say she was robbed or raped or what?" "I don't know son her parents said the police don't know right now what happened."

"Mom please give her parents my sympathy, I need to get to my wife."

"Ok love call me soon ok and tell Vanessa we love her and will see her soon." Jarvis hangs up and now has confirmation that Sheka is really dead.

Jarvis calls Tranetta but gets no answer.

"Tranetta call me as soon as you get this message." Tranetta is in bed with Andre who happened to just be in her neighborhood and decided to drop in for a little quiet time. Tranetta totally ignores Jarvis call.

“So miss Tranetta what are your plans for today?” Tranetta decides to drop a bomb on Andre with a shocking response.

“Well, I thought I would start by telling your wife I’m pregnant, and then maybe get some sun at the beach who knows.” Andre is about to fall over from Tranetta’s nasty sarcasm.

“What the fuck did you just say?” Tranetta getting out of bed and standing directly in front of Andre she gets bold and nasty.

"You heard me or do I need to get you a hearing aid Motherfucker?"

"Tranetta you have no idea who you fucking with little girl, you might come up missing so slow your row."

"Oh is that a threat am I suppose to be scared?"

"No I don't make threats I make promises so you just better keep your threats to yourself and far as my wife is concerned you would have to find her first or did you forget we moved."

"I bet you thought I was going to be your fool forever huh Andre? Well I have news for you first of all I don't scare easy and second if you want me to keep my mouth shut you better start filling my pockets cause I know exactly where you and the lovely wife lives."

"I don't believe you are pregnant you lying your ass off girl trying to trap a brother girl please try something else."

"Really Andre I don't think so."

Tranetta goes in the bathroom and come out what the positive pregnancy test she stole from the trash when Vanessa took the test.

“So what now Andre I guess this test is lying too huh?’ Andre looks at the stick and back at Tranetta with a weird look on his face.

“Awe man, Tranetta I thought you were on something. Besides this don’t mean shit, I know it’s not mine so how about you go tell the real daddy.”

“I was on birth control but something must have went wrong, I really wasn’t trying to get pregnant this is your baby and you will take responsibility.”

“How you know where we live?”

“I figured it out Andre you not dealing with a dummy you know.”

“What the hell you gonna do? I mean I know you not going to keep it are you?” “Well I’m not going to kill it.”

“Look Tranetta I don’t want any more kids man.”

“Looks like you are about to be a daddy again.” Tranetta looking at Andre and knowing she has control now. Tranetta is ruthless enough to go through with it and bleed Andre for every dime she can possibly get out of him. Andre gives Tranetta a look of disgust and walks towards to door then turns to Tranetta.

“I don’t care what you do, I am out of here.

"Hold on Andre if you think you are going to just walk away you have another thing coming. I will make sure your little wife knows the whole story." Andre walks to Tranetta grabs her and backs her into the wall.

"You dirty tramp, if you breathe one word of this lie to my wife I will take care of you and I promise you slut no one will ever find you. I don't believe its mine anyway, you lucky I offered you money for an abortion but now you can forget it. I don't want you do you understand me? Now as I said before I am out of here deal with this shit on your own." Andre walks out and slams the door behind him. Tranetta is livid because her plan didn't work on Andre.

"That no good dirty dog, dam, I guess now I have to stick with Jarvis plan. I can't stand Jarvis; I know I can't trust him he may try to get rid of me so I better play it cool just in case I have to beat him to the punch." Tranetta has an evil look in her eyes.

Jarvis is back at the hospital playing the loving husband. The doctor walks in and tells Vanessa and Jarvis that all the test have checked out and Vanessa can go home in the morning providing that she only rest no strenuous activities, she is to go to doctor's appointments and back to bed rest only. Jarvis thanks the doctor and looks over to Vanessa.

"See told you everything will be alright, now you heard the doctor bed rest for you my love." Vanessa looks deep into Jarvis eyes and plays along with him. "Thanks for being such a wonderful husband I don't know what I would do without you." Jarvis leans in and gives Vanessa a kiss.

"I have to go to get groceries because there is not a thing in the fridge, plus I need to do laundry and clean the place for my lovely wife I would not want you to come home to a big mess so I will be here early to get you ok."

"Ok baby, I can't wait to get home and I sure will be happy when this baby comes." Jarvis walks out without telling Vanessa about Sheka. Vanessa is thinking how can she find out everything that is going on. The whole idea of what Jarvis whispered to her just doesn't make sense. However, Vanessa is not in the mood to trust anymore, feeling used by the world Vanessa is learning how to play hard ball and now is willing to show them all how to play the game.

Jarvis returns back home to call Tranetta. "Hello Jarvis, what you need?" "Vanessa is coming home tomorrow and I need you to get back close to her so she can feel comfortable while I work my magic."

"Yeah right, you know she may not be willing to do that."

"Sure she will she needs all the friends she can get right now."

"Ok if you say so. What you want me to do?"

"For starters I want you to go to the hospital and see her and let her know how much you care about her, can you do that for me baby?"

"Ok I will give me an hour."

"Cool, I need to get everything straighten up here so she will feel comfortable." "Alright, I will talk to you later Jarvis bye." Tranetta is not feeling this but she decides that she must do what she has to in order to get paid.

Tarnetta has arrived at the hospital. "Hey Vanessa sweetie." Vanessa has a confused look on her face.

"Listen, Jarvis told me you were in the hospital and I wanted to come and apologize for my behavior, I was completely out of line. I really miss you girl, you know how we used to talk and share things, laughing into the wee hours of the morning?

I am so happy for you. Jarvis told me the wedding was so beautiful, I was kicking myself because I was not there. Can you forgive me for being a crazy bitch?"

Vanessa gives Tranetta a look and then holds her hands out to Tranetta for a hug.

"Of course I forgive you girl, I miss you too. I have been feeling bad since we had that altercation."

"Well, now that's all out the way, how are you doing?"

"I feel like a stuffed pig, but other than that I feel great."

"What happened that landed you here in this fabulous hotel?"

"I wouldn't call this fabulous but, I just got sick, my blood pressure went up and before I knew it I was here."

"Well, worry no more your best friend is here to help you from now on."

"Thanks Tranetta this means so much to me, to have you and I speaking again."

"So where is Jarvis?"

"He went home to clean his mess before I get there tomorrow."

"Girl you are so lucky to have a good husband like Jarvis, I wish I could find someone that sweet."

"What happened to Andre I thought you guys were tight."

"He is a loser, I found out things about him that I was not willing to deal with."

"So, what about Odell?"

"You know he went back to school close to home so he could be with his mama." "Oh well you will find someone soon enough."

"I know and he will be the one. Listen, Vanessa I have to run. I want to visit with you so I can help you out. I need to get your address. Here I will save it in my phone."

"It's 12784 Honey Well Drive; do you know how to get there?"

"I can map quest it, so I will see you tomorrow if you want company."

"Call me and we will take it from there my number is still the same." Tranetta gives Vanessa a hug and leaves. Tranetta already knows where Vanessa and Jarvis lives she is the one who has left the notes.

Its time for Vanessa to go home, Vanessa is sitting ready and patiently on

Jarvis to arrive. "Good morning my dear wife, are you ready to go home?"

"Yes, I am more then ready, hit that call button baby and let the nurse know we are ready." The nurse comes in with a wheel chair and Vanessa prescriptions and orders from the doctor.

"It is so good to be home."

As Vanessa walks into her lovely home. "Ok Vanessa let's get you in bed like the doctor ordered." Jarvis helps Vanessa upstairs to bed where he can have full control.

"I am at your service love, do you need anything?"

"No, I think I will just get some rest."

"Ok, if you need me I will be in my office working." Jarvis leans in and gives Vanessa a kiss on her forehead and leaves the room.

"I wonder what he's up to being so nice now, but when I was unconscious he was hoping I died, what's up with that?"

Tranetta calls Jarvis to see what's up with Vanessa.

"Is she home yet?"

"Yes"

"Can I come by?"

"Not today maybe tomorrow she is resting now."

"So what's our next move Jarvis?"

"We are just waiting now for the baby to be born, and then we will take it from there."

"This shit is taking too much time; I need this BITCH gone forever so we can get that money."

"Calm down Tranetta, it will all happen just be patient. We will be rolling in more money then we can spend. Especially, now that Sheka is out of the picture." "Yeah, have you heard anything else on the case?"

"No I did talk to her parents and her funeral is next week."

"Are you going?"

"Of course, you know I have to show up for the occasion."

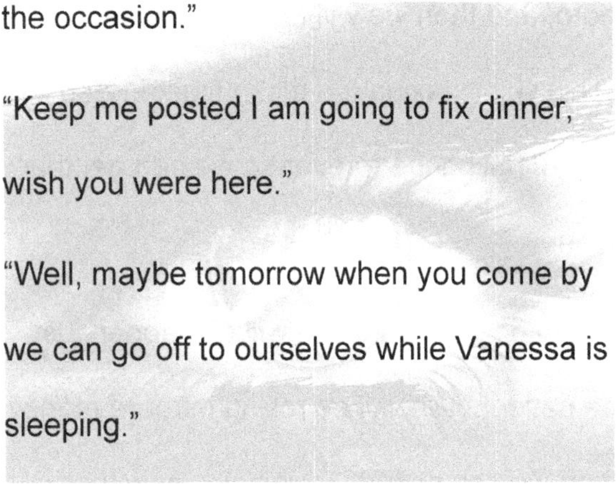

"Keep me posted I am going to fix dinner, wish you were here."

"Well, maybe tomorrow when you come by we can go off to ourselves while Vanessa is sleeping."

"Why not now nothing like the present."

"No I have some work to finish but tomorrow I promise."

"Oh, ok see you tomorrow bye." Jarvis hangs up from Tranetta to go check on Vanessa. When Jarvis opens the bedroom door Vanessa is on the phone with her Mother getting the news about Sheka.

"Mama, are you sure Sheka is dead? I can't believe it, what happened? Please give my condolences to her family and I am going to try and make the funeral next week." Vanessa hangs up from her mother, although, Sheka and Vanessa had their differences Vanessa still feels sorrow in her heart.

"Baby is everything ok?"

"Jarvis, someone killed Sheka in her home."

"I know baby it's a tragedy."

"You knew about this and didn't tell me."

"I didn't want to upset you baby I was waiting until you were home a few days."

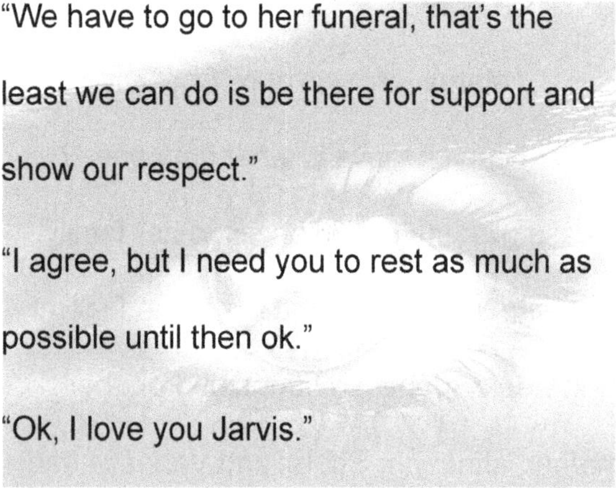

"We have to go to her funeral, that's the least we can do is be there for support and show our respect."

"I agree, but I need you to rest as much as possible until then ok."

"Ok, I love you Jarvis."

"I love you too baby, is there anything you want?"

"Yes how about a big bowl of ice cream."

"At your service we have some in the fridge, we have butter pecan, strawberry & your favorite vanilla. So which one do you prefer?"

"I will have my favorite, vanilla."

"Vanilla it is." Jarvis goes into the kitchen ad scoops ice cream into bowls for him and Vanessa.

"How's your ice cream love?"

"This is the best bowl of ice cream I have ever had. You are the best husband in the world."

"Stop it you making my head big girl." They both laugh, then Jarvis finish his ice cream and heads back to the office. Vanessa is thinking what a fraud Jarvis is when all of a sudden it hits Vanessa that she has inherited a large sum of money and that can be the reason for Jarvis marrying her. The only thing that is keeping Jarvis from the money is it is in a safe account. But at the same time she is wondering how Jarvis would know because the only person she told was Sheka. Vanessa grabs her mouth thinking what if Jarvis killed Sheka but quickly dismiss that because she can't see Jarvis doing anything so horrible or could he and besides, Jarvis was with her when it happened.

The next day Jarvis awaken Vanessa with a kiss and a hug. "Baby, I need to run out for a little while and take care of some business, will you be ok for a couple of hours? I promise I won't be long and when I get back I will fix you a delicious dinner. Before I leave I am going to make you your favorite breakfast waffles." Jarvis is in the kitchen and decide to call Tranetta to come over until he gets back.

"Baby I need you to come over and sit with Vanessa; I need to take care of some business."

"I'm on my way."

"Thanks Tranetta." Jarvis comes back with a tray of buttery waffles for Vanessa to enjoy.

"Tranetta is going to come over and stay with you, she told me you guys were cool again and I assumed you would not mind if she came by."

"No problem I would love to have her company."

"Good I'm running late I got to get showered and out the door." Jarvis showered and dressed running out the door when he opens the door Tranetta was just about to ring the door bell.

"Hey you don't you look handsome."

"Shh, Vanessa is right upstairs." Jarvis gives Tranetta a quick kiss and leaves. Tranetta goes upstairs with Vanessa.

"Hey Nessa look at your face girl you are glowing."

"Hey girl, I'm glad you came I can use the company."

"So how is everything going with you and your wonderful husband?"

"It's cool he is a big help I can get use to his spoiling me."

"Girl, I know that's right every woman deserves to be spoiled. Vanessa is there anything I can get for you?"

"No don't put yourself out your company is comforting enough."

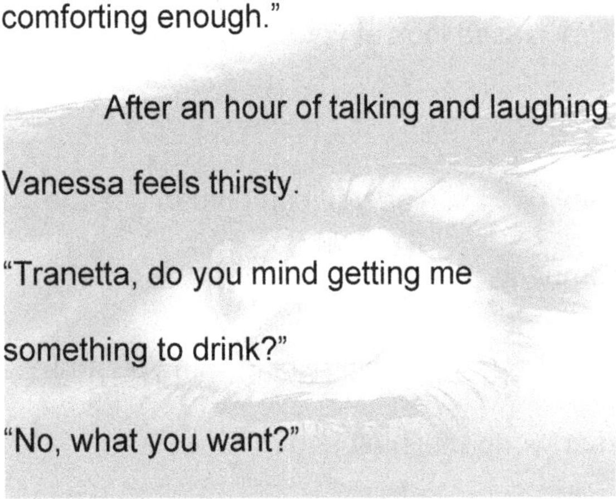

After an hour of talking and laughing Vanessa feels thirsty.

"Tranetta, do you mind getting me something to drink?"

"No, what you want?"

"I am really craving for a strawberry milk shake."

"I can run to the diner up the street is that ok?"

"Yes, and make it a large."

"You got it I will be right back, oh when I lock the door I am going to need your key to get back in."

"Look over on the dresser; it's the one with my initial on it." Tranetta grabs Vanessa keys and head out. As Tranetta is driving she see a place to make a copy of Vanessa house key and stops to get a copy. "This is too easy, now I have your house key slut I think I will drop by anytime." Tranetta has this devious look on her face as she leaves the store with a copy of Vanessa's key.

Tranetta gets back into her car with the shakes and decides to put a little knock out drop in Vanessa's. "This should hold her for a minute, this way I can check out a few things around the house and see what's up with Jarvis ass." Tranetta calls out to Vanessa as she enters the house. "Vanessa I'm back" Tranetta enters the room and hands Vanessa her shake.

"One large strawberry milk shake to quench your cravings mama."

"Thank you this looks delicious, what kind do you have?"

"I got the pine apple, and it's good too." Vanessa is half way through her milk shake when she begins to feel drowsy. Tranetta watching her closely as Vanessa drifts off and drops her shake to the floor. Tranetta walks over to Vanessa to make sure she is out, cleans up the spill from the shake, places Vanessa keys back on the dresser and then walks into Jarvis office to snoop to see what she can find. Tranetta finds statements of deposits and the will Vanessa grandmother left leaving Vanessa well paid.

Tranetta eyes light up like a Christmas tree. "Oh yea that's it money, money, money I can't wait to get my hands on this. Now that I know how much is at stake I can get it all if I get can get rid of Vanessa, marry Jarvis then take care of him. I will never have any money worries ever again. That bastard didn't tell me it was this much and the brat has money coming too" Tranetta is excited and ready to get this show on the road.

Jarvis comes back a little earlier than Tranetta expected she hears him and carefully put her findings back in place, runs into the room pretending she is sleeping too. Jarvis comes upstairs and find his girls sleeping. Tranetta awakens and looks at Vanessa. "Hey Jarvis I guess we must have fallen asleep after those milkshakes. How about you and I get in a little coziness of our own while sleeping beauty here rest?" Jarvis is definitely game for a little love in the afternoon as he takes Tranetta into the guest room where they make hot and heavy love as Vanessa is sleeping. "Girl you know just what a brother needs now, let's get out of here before Vanessa wakes up and catch us." "Oh I think she is good and tired she should be sleeping for a minute that milkshake and all that laughing has her pooped." Tranetta and Jarvis gets dressed and Tranetta heads home.

"Tell Vanessa I said to call me."

"Yeah you just stick to the plan baby." They kiss at the door and Jarvis heads back upstairs to see if Vanessa is awake.

Vanessa is up and going to the bathroom but feels very groogy.

“Hey sleepy head what you doing up?”

“I need to go to the bathroom, I feel so lazy.”

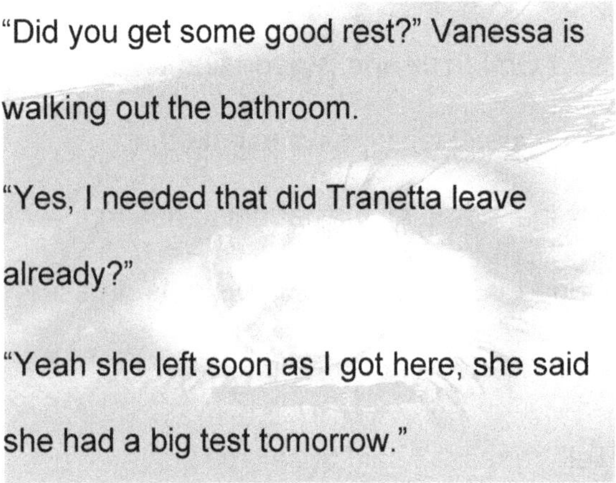

“Did you get some good rest?” Vanessa is walking out the bathroom.

“Yes, I needed that did Tranetta leave already?”

“Yeah she left soon as I got here, she said she had a big test tomorrow.”

“I am missing a lot of school.” “I already talked with your professors and the administration and they are going to give me your assignments.”

"Good I can't get too behind in my studies that would just take me longer to finish and I want to finish as soon as possible."

"I know baby and you will, you are a very smart woman I believe you will get it done." Jarvis smiles at Vanessa. "Can I get you something? I am about to prepare a good dinner for you."

"Really and what is chef J going to make for us tonight?"

"I thought I would surprise you, so hold on sit back and relax here's a bell if you need me. I am off to cook my love." Vanessa gives Jarvis a little grin and turns the television on.

Its one month later Sunday morning four a.m. and Vanessa awakens Jarvis to heavy cramps in her back.

“Jarvis wake up I am in terrible pain I think its time.” Jarvis jumps up calls Dr. Ross who tells him to meet them in labor and delivery. Jarvis picks Vanessa up and heads out the door.

“Hurry J its getting harder.” They make it to the hospital and Vanessa water breaks just as they get to the room. The anesthesiologist comes in and gives Vanessa an epidural to help ease the pain.

"Is the pain better sweetie?"

"Yes thank God for epidural." Tranetta walks in frantic.

"Girl you better not have this baby without me, thank you Jarvis for calling me I would not have missed this for the world."

"I knew you and Vanessa would want you here, so thank you for coming." The nurse comes in to check Vanessa to see how far along she is. "I better get the Doctor you are ready." The team comes in and set up for the delivery of the baby. Jarvis has called their parents and have everyone on speaker phone so they can be part of the baby entering the world.

The Doctor tells Vanessa to push one more time. Vanessa gives it everything she has in her and finally a beautiful 8 lb 3 oz. baby boy enters the world and everyone is ecstatic. You can hear the joy of the grand parents and others on the phone. Jarvis gives Vanessa a big kiss and hugs. Tranetta turns to Vanessa smiling. "Vanessa he's beautiful, I am so happy for you and Jarvis." Vanessa is exhausted from the delivery.

Vanessa is into her room where flowers are being delivered. Jarvis and Tranetta is marveling over the baby. "So

Jarvis what are you guys going to name him?"

"Girl you better recognize, you know he is a junior." Vanessa is smiling and wants to rest.

"Well, that's ok by me as long as I can get some rest now I am exhausted. I didn't know having a baby was so much work."

"That's my que girl once again congratulations on your bundle of joy I need to get out of here but I will be back tomorrow sweetie ok, call me if you need me for anything."

"Hold up Tranetta I will walk you to your car. I will be right back baby ok." Tranetta and Jarvis get into the elevator. Jarvis turns to Tranetta with excitement. "Baby we are about to get paid I am so glad it's a boy because that raises the stakes."

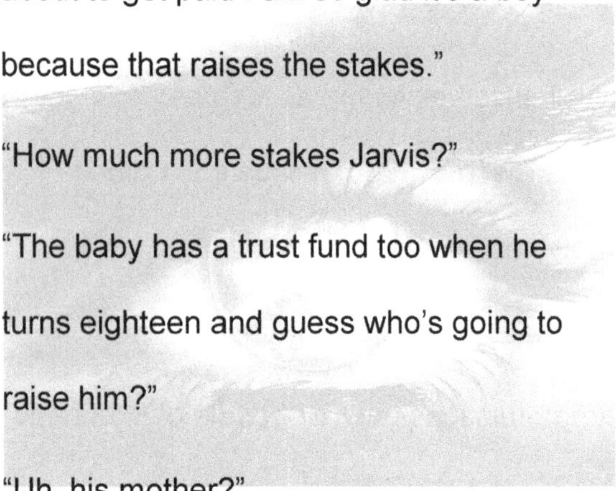

"How much more stakes Jarvis?"

"The baby has a trust fund too when he turns eighteen and guess who's going to raise him?"

"Uh, his mother?"

"No my love you too funny, of course you and I. We have to kill Vanessa so I can get the life insurance and the money from the will it states that if anything happens to Vanessa the surviving spouse inherits the money. Now that info we have to thank Ms. Sheka for that's why she was so hell bent on getting her cut." "Well we don't have to worry about her cut anymore cause she is history." The elevator door opens and Jarvis stays on and tells Tranetta he will see her later tonight for a little action and how they will plan Vanessa's accident.

"So Jarvis I will see you about nine."

"Yes as soon as visiting hours are over I want you to meet me at the house." "What about my curfew?"

"Tell Ms. Felicia you have an emergency and will have to be out."

"Good call see you at the house."

Once again Jarvis goes back to Vanessa to play the good husband. "Hey baby I am the proud father of this beautiful baby boy." Vanessa is sleeping and does not hear a word Jarvis is saying. Jarvis sits until visiting hours are over. He wakes Vanessa to tell her he is leaving and will see her tomorrow. Jarvis gives Vanessa a kiss and is off to meet with Tranetta.

Tranetta pulls into the driveway same time as Jarvis they join hands and walk into the house.

"Can I get you some wine Ms. Tranetta so we can toast Vanessa for making us very rich."

"Yes please, so, how does it feel to be a father?"

"it feels so good especially, a rich father. Now, we must play this out very carefully. Of course you know we can't move too fast because we don't want anyone getting suspicious." Tranetta gets irritated at Jarvis comment.

"How long do we have to wait or should I say how long do I have to wait?"

"Calm down girl it's not going to be that long, at least let the baby get a few months old."

"A few months, I think you stringing me along, now Jarvis don't bullshit me on this or you will find yourself in a crunch you get my drift?"

"Tranetta, baby I wouldn't do that to you." Jarvis gets closer to Tranetta and kiss her. "come on baby lets go upstairs." Tranetta seems to calm down and take Jarvis up on his intriguing offer for love.

The next morning Tranetta wakes up in Jarvis arms and Vanessa's bed with the lingering of Jarvis all night romance.

Tranetta turns to Jarvis to give him one last taste of love before they leave for their day of deceit and lies to keep Vanessa in the dark.

Jarvis is sitting with Vanessa watching the baby and wondering to himself how lucky he is to be able to pull off his game. However, Vanessa has a game of her own and holding this secret is something she never thought she would have to do. The nurse walks in to take Vanessa's vitals just to make sure everything is going well. "Looks as though you will be able to go home tomorrow Vanessa everything seems to be normal, are you having any pain?" "No I feel great.'

"The Doctor will be in soon and he can make the call whether you will be able to leave or not ok."

"I hope so I am ready to get home."

"Do you need anything before I go?"

"No thank you."

"Baby thank you for this wonderful son he is so precious I can barely take my eyes off him."

"Jarvis put the baby down you are going to have him spoiled before he can get home."

"I can't help myself he is already a little man; I promise I am going to be the best father this child could ever ask for."

"Have you seen Tranetta today?" "No why?" "Just asking she said she was coming to visit today." Before Vanessa could say another word Tranetta pops her head in the door.

"He girl how are you and this fine baby doing today? Look I brought him a little something." Vanessa is eager to see what's in the gift bag.

"Tranetta it's beautiful where you found this little Texas jersey."

"Girl you know I got the hook up."

"Thanks Tranetta this is very sweet of you."

"I plan on spoiling him because you know I am his God Mother right?"

"Of course I can't think of a better God Mother than you."

"Jarvis let me hold him you over here spoiling the baby and won't let him go." Tranetta is holding the baby and thinking what a meal ticket he is for her. She plans on taking Jarvis out the picture as soon as she can get Vanessa out of the equation as well.

The next day Jarvis is at the hospital ready to take his family home. "Dr. Ross I appreciate everything you have done for me and the baby." "No problems Vanessa just make sure you take this medicine if you experience any pain and also don't forget your follow up appointment. Have you thought about what type of birth control you will take? If you would like the Deprovera injection we can administer that right now and every three months after."

"I heard about that and sure I want to try it."

"Ok I can have the nurse come right in and then you can be on your way."

"Finally, home at last I can get some real food." "What you want baby I can run out and pick up something."

"That would be great and you can fill my prescription plus get the baby a case of milk. So how about some burgers, fries and a milkshake you know my favorite." Jarvis walks over to Vanessa and gently grab her around her waist.

"You are my favorite and now that lil Jarvis is here he is my favorite too." Jarvis gives Vanessa a peck on the lips and out the door to the supermarket and burger hut.

Tranetta is calling Jarvis as he is turning into the supermarket parking lot. "What's up baby girl you miss me already."

"Yes I do where you at?" "At the supermarket getting lil J some formula why what's up?"

"I'm just seeing how everything is going."

"Awe that's sweet, you know you're my girl right."

"I better be all the trouble I have been through for you." Jarvis gives a chuckle. "Listen Tranetta I need to get this stuff. When I'm finished I will give you a call." "Ok daddy I will look forward to hearing from you." In the meantime Vanessa makes sure the baby is snug in his crib then begins to look through Jarvis things. Vanessa comes up on the will and financial statements and some more papers that Jarvis has been hiding from her.

"This bastard has been using my credit cards. How the hell did he get my credit cards? Oh my God my visa is maxed out." Vanessa can hardly believe Jarvis is stealing from her. Vanessa snoops farther and find that Jarvis has a two million dollar life insurance policy on her that he didn't tell her about. Vanessa is finding out a lot of stuff he has hidden away including condoms and other women phone numbers.

"Honey I'm back come get your food before it gets cold." "Ok baby here I come." Vanessa is livid but decides to play it off and see all of what is going on she intends to get to the root of all this wickedness.

"There she is looking as beautiful as ever, I think I got everything on your list." "You did, I was just putting lil J in his crib. I sure am hungry." Vanessa tears into her burger as though she is starving. "Thanks J this is so good and the vanilla shake tops it right off." "You are so welcome my love anything for you. Vanessa I never apologized to you for being a jerk the day you got sick. So much was going on it got delayed but, I am telling you now I was wrong and I apologize do you forgive me?"

"Of course silly I been forgave you now let's finish our dinner and maybe we can catch a movie while the baby is sleeping."

"I'm sorry baby I promise TJ I would come over and look at the paperwork for the café."

"Can it wait until tomorrow?"

"I wish but he and his wife is going out of town for a couple of weeks and we need to get it prepared for my meeting with the investors on Wednesday. I'm sorry baby I promise to make it short so I can get back home soon ok."

"Ok I guess you have to do what you have to do."

"See that's why I married you because you're not just beautiful but understanding, I love you for that." Jarvis finishes his meal and gives Vanessa a quick kiss.

"I will be back soon as I can, call me if you need me I will come right away ok baby see you in a few."

"Good glad that bastard gone he interrupted my investigation, I could care less if he never came back." Vanessa goes back to her search finding all sorts of secrets Jarvis has been keeping from her.

Jarvis pulls into the campus and gives Tranetta a call to let her know he is outside.

"Come in baby the door is open." Travis walks through the door to find Tranetta on the sofa naked.

"Now that's the kind of greeting I like, pose for me baby." Tranetta opens her legs to expose her goodies and Jarvis falls to his knees and goes to work. After some hot sneaky love Jarvis and Tranetta discuss their evil plans for Vanessa.

"Vanessa I'm back where are you baby?" "I'm in the nursery feeding the baby." Jarvis walks upstairs to join his wife and baby.

"Look at you feeding our son and looking so good doing it. I am going to let you do your thing, I need to shower. I will meet you in the bedroom. Too bad I can't hit that right now or you would be all mine with your fine self." Vanessa continues feeding the baby as though Jarvis hadn't said a word. Vanessa is thinking "Right, you may never be able to hit this again you fraud."

It's been three months and lil J is getting huge and Tranetta's patience is getting short. The house has been filled with family and friends. Vanessa's mother and father just left yesterday after a month stay which makes Jarvis a happy man because he couldn't see Tranetta the way he wanted to.

"Our house is back to normal again, I love my parents but they were driving me crazy." "They weren't that bad Vanessa, plus they were a lot of help including Tiffy she is proud to be an aunt. Now, my parents they really drove me crazy. My mom was ordering me around like I was the help

Jarvis do this, Jarvis do that." They both laugh as Jarvis walks over to the wine cooler to get a bottle of wine. "So my darling wife you think I can finally interest you in some hot sweaty sex?" "Not tonight J I am so tired, maybe tomorrow night when I rest some I'm going to bed." Vanessa precedes upstairs leaving Jarvis alone in he living room with his manhood un satisfied. Jarvis is not happy with Vanessa's daily excuses and decides to take a drive. Jarvis decides he wants a little adventure in his life so he goes to a strip club where the women are plentiful and ready to give in to his demands.

Jarvis sits at the bar and order a double scotch when a beautiful slender but shapely young woman walks over to him. "So what does a handsome man like you desire tonight?" "Well, I am looking for something as beautiful as yourself, are you available for a one on one?" "I'm available for whatever you want." "Fair enough how about we take this party to the private room."

"Of course you know that will cost you."

"How much?"

"To start a hundred if you want longer its fifty every hour."

"Then let's do two hours."

"Let's go big boy." The woman leads Jarvis upstairs so they can have some alone time. Jarvis has satisfied his cravings and back to the house he goes when Tranetta calls and Jarvis just ignores her call for now.

Vanessa is sleeping when Jarvis enters the bedroom. Jarvis quietly moves around the room trying not to wake Vanessa. Although, Vanessa is awake only playing as though she is still sleeping. Jarvis goes in to shower. Vanessa is wondering where Jarvis has been since it is three a.m. but Vanessa decides to just let it ride for now because she plans on beating him at this game he thinks he is scheming her with.

The next morning Vanessa is up making breakfast when Jarvis comes into the kitchen and grabs her from behind kissing her on the neck.

“Good morning my black queen.”

“Good morning to you.” Lil Jarvis wakes up crying to get his breakfast as well. Jarvis quickly goes upstairs to get the baby and comes back to breakfast. Vanessa is smiling at her bouncing baby boy as she sets the table and gets him a bottle. Vanessa sits down as Jarvis is feeding the baby.

"So honey what are your plans for today?" Jarvis looks up and smiles at Vanessa. "Well sweetie I thought the three of us could have a picnic in the park. I can make some sandwiches, get some drinks and we just make a family day. How does that sound?"

"Sounds great to me, I think some fresh air will do us all some good." "Then its settled after breakfast I will go to the store and pick up some things for our fun day in the park."

Jarvis is driving to the store when he sees Tranetta heading his way. Jarvis blows his horn and stops to talk to Tranetta. "Girl where are you going so fast?"

"Over to your house to see Vanessa and the baby. Where are you going?"

"On my way to the store me, Vanessa and the baby are going to have a picnic in the park."

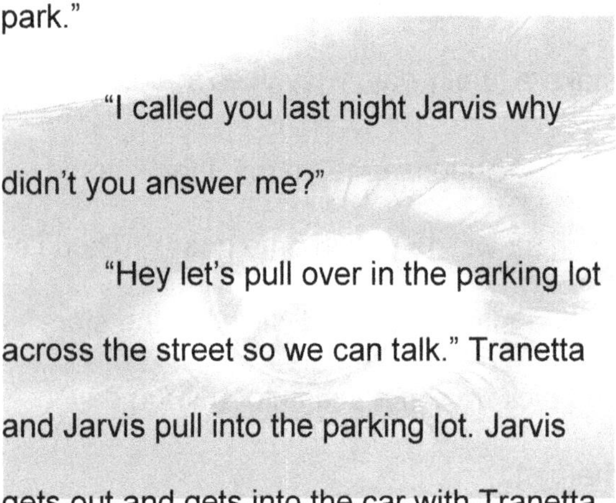

"I called you last night Jarvis why didn't you answer me?"

"Hey let's pull over in the parking lot across the street so we can talk." Tranetta and Jarvis pull into the parking lot. Jarvis gets out and gets into the car with Tranetta. "Before you start tripping Tranetta, we were exhausted from the last of a lot of company so we went to bed early sorry I didn't get your call."

"Look Jarvis I have been waiting long enough my patience is wearing thin. When are we going to take care of Vanessa?"

"Soon baby I promise you just have to be a little more patient it is all about to come into play."

"You think Vanessa suspects anything J?"

"No she is in the dark she will never know what hit her. So why don't you go and pay your little visit like the best friend and let me handle the details."

"Ok I will be there when you get there so hurry up." Jarvis gets out of Tranetta car and heads to the store and Traneta to Jarvis and Vanessa's house when she gets a call from Andre.

"What the hell do you want Andre?"

"I am just checking on you to see if you are alright. Tranetta I been thinking. I don't want to treat you bad, are you still pregnant?"

"No I had an abortion because you can't love me like I need to be loved."

"Well, that's a weight off my shoulders. So now we can both move on, I hope you telling me the truth, besides neither one of us need a baby anyway so I guess we good"

"That's cool with me and if there is nothing else I have things to do so good bye Andre." Tranetta hangs up her phone as she is pulling into Vanessa's drive way.

Vanessa opens the door to greet Tranetta. "Tranetta come in its good to see you again girl."

"I was in the neighborhood and thought I would drop in and she my favorite family. Where's my baby?"

"He's sleeping would you like some coffee? I just finished brewing a fresh pot."

"Yes please, I would love a cup you know how I like it."

Vanessa heads into the kitchen and Tranetta have a seat at the dining room table looking around in envy at Vanessa's beautiful wall coverings.

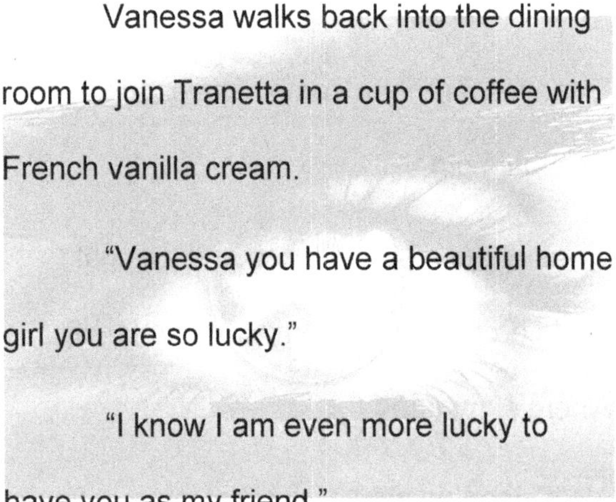

Vanessa walks back into the dining room to join Tranetta in a cup of coffee with French vanilla cream.

"Vanessa you have a beautiful home girl you are so lucky."

"I know I am even more lucky to have you as my friend."

"Where's Jarvis?"

"He went to the store to get some things we are going to the park for a picnic."

"That sounds like fun."

"Are you busy if not you can join us I'm sure Jarvis won't mind."

"Maybe some other time I have some things to do today."

"Ok well at least I tried." Just then Jarvis walks in with bags for their day in the park. Jarvis says hello to Tranetta and goes to start making sandwiches.

"Thanks for the coffee Vanessa I better get out of here."

"Do you have to leave so soon."

"Yea I got to get to my chores and take care of some business."

Vanessa walks Tranetta to the door. Jarvis comes to say good bye to Tranetta and when she hugs Vanessa she throws a kiss and a wink Jarvis way. Jarvis just smiles and Tranetta leaves. Tranetta text Jarvis with a little sexy message that she will be naked at nine if he can get away from his ball and chain.

"I think I have everything in the basket."

"Good I will get lil J and the blankets."

Jarvis stops Vanessa to give her a kiss and as she walks away he gives her a little pat on the butt.

Some time has passed and everything seems to be going good Jarvis is now starting to plan getting rid of Vanessa. He now feels enough time has passed. Lil J is almost a year old and with him walking it makes things easier. Tranetta is happy to know what Jarvis has planned and she is ready and waiting.

Jarvis and Vanessa are out enjoying a day at the outdoor market; Tranetta lets herself in with her key she made a while back. Tranetta goes into the living room and starts to dance around as though this is her home, looking at photographs, admiring

Vanessa and Jarvis elegant taste. She goes into the kitchen looking in cabinets, opens the refrigerator, slams the door and leans up against it with a sour look on her face.

Tranetta hears car doors close and gets frantic but quickly remembers she parked on the next street. Vanessa comes in with Jarvis behind her holding the baby. Tranetta quiet, but, quickly exits to the back of the house and goes into the sunroom. Vanessa has a weird feeling that someone is there. Vanessa walks to the dining room where Jarvis is and tells him her suspicion

"Calm down baby I will check the house out you take the baby and go into the living room and stay there if you here anything strange call the police." Jarvis then starts with the closets, goes upstairs and clears the area , then he heads downstairs to the back of the house and enters into the sunroom Tranetta is hiding behind some big boxes by the window, when she accidentally knocks over a vase.

"Who the hell is there come out or you gonna get some hot lead. Tranetta comes from around the boxes with her hands up. Vanessa hollers from the kitchen.

"Jarvis are you alright?"

"Yea baby its all clear take the baby upstairs and get him ready for bed."

"Ok you sure."

"Yes Vanessa I will be up in a minute."

"Ok baby I'm going upstairs can you take the steaks out. I will be back down to start dinner as soon as I get J settled down."

"I got you nessa." Jarvis looks at Tranetta with an evil look.

"What the hell you doing in my house Tranetta?"

"Stop tripping J I was jogging pass and saw your door was open and came in to make sure everything was ok when I heard a noise and hid. You should be thanking me."

"Dam, Vanessa must have left the door open again when she was rushing man, this girl is getting on my last nerve."

"Since we are here I think it would be exciting to get a little while Vanessa is rocking the baby I can be rocking you." Tranetta pulls her panties down and her dress up to show Jarvis her goods. Jarvis eyes are locked on Tranetta as she moves around sexy. Jarvis walks over to Tranetta unzipping his pants and takes her right there with Vanessa upstairs.

After Jarvis and Tranetta little quickie Jarvis sneaks Tranetta out the side door and tells her that it's time to get

Vanessa out the picture. Tranetta kisses Jarvis on the forehead and leaves. Jarvis walks into the kitchen and takes out the steaks as though Tranetta was never there.

Tranetta walks to her door and starts to unlock it when she is startled by Andre standing there.

"Andre is that you?"

"Yea baby it's me can we talk?"

"No Andre I have had a long day and don't need any company, go home to your lil wife and kids." Tranetta blows him off and goes in for the night. After entering her dwelling Tranetta could hear strange sounds coming from where Andre was standing. Looking out of her window only to see Andre storm off in a hurry.

The morning air is fresh as it hits Tranetta face from the open bedroom window, Tranetta is in deep thought as she lays in bed longer than usual trying to come up with the perfect plan to get rid of Vanessa. Then all of a sudden it hits Tranetta "I think I will tell J to get a hit man I know just who can get the job done." Tranetta calls Jarvis with her idea.

"Hello"

"Hey J I need to speak to you I have the perfect plan."

"Oh really, and what would that be?"

"Just meet me later and I will run it by you and see what you think."

"Yea stay where you are I will be over in about an hour, because the time has come."

"I will be here."

Vanessa is up tending to the baby when Andre comes in and tells her he has a business meeting.

"But it Sunday Jarvis what type of business are you doing on a Sunday morning?"

Jarvis is irritated at Vanessa questioning him about his business. Hi Jarvis turns and looks at Vanessa with an angry stare, his gaze lingered there for a second nonetheless. He rose to his feet and began pacing. In his anger he knocks a glass from the night table next to the bed. The glass scrunched under his feet. “Why are you in my dam business Vanessa?”

“Why do you have such an attitude Jarvis? What you got something to hide?”

Jarvis quickly walks over to Vanessa and grab her back the neck and slams her against the wall with fierce anger.

“Don’t you ever question me do you hear me Vanessa I don’t need this shit I’m out.”

Jarvis lets Vanessa go and storms downstairs and out the door to Tranetta's

Vanessa is shocked at Jarvis temper and slides down the wall and cries. Jarvis had someone in mind for the job as well as he thinks to himself about his options, when really there was no other option. He didn't like it, but this was why you always kept a favour or two in your wallet should things get screwed up. But still, he'd rather big favours like that remain in his wallet. Jarvis arrives at Tranetta's with his plan clearly mapped out.

"Listen Tranetta its got to be done and soon Vanessa is getting hard to bear she is beginning to wear me thin. I know a guy that can do this for us he's very professional and his work is clean and quick."

"I'm so excited to hear that Jarvis because that is what I wanted to talk to you about, getting somebody to do the job, now, if your man don't work I know someone as equally good. Then once this is all over we can be together." Jarvis looks at Tranetta with a weary look and beginning thinking quietly. He took the phone from his pocket, and began to dial. It took only one ring of the phone for the man to answer.

"I was wondering when this day would come." The man's voice was gravely, but by no means sounded like someone who had been awoken unexpectedly in the early hours.

Jarvis didn't say a word.

"So, what'll it be? Something big I'm guessing." Jarvis hated the cheerfulness of the man's voice.

His eyes remained fixed on the door. "I need a get out clause, Bob." He had to force the words from his mouth.

"You? Never thought I'd see the day."

Neither had he.

"Look, you're going to need to make this happen quickly."

"No problem I only need the stats and when you want it to happen, and of course about a hundred thousand with fifty deposit and fifty when its done."

"Where can we meet?"

"Is this your number I can reach you at?"

"Yes"

"Then I will contact you in a day or so and when you come make sure you bring the money or the deal is off."

"No problem I will be where ever you say with the money."

Jarvis hangs up the phone with Tranetta close upon him , wanting to know what's going on.

"So what did he say?"

"He will call in a day with a meet up time, He also wants a fifty thousand dollar deposit and fifty when its done."

"So he wants a hundred thousand dollars?"

"Yep"

"So you got that kind of money?"

"You shouldn't worry about that I will get it."

"I better get home. I need you to just hang in with me baby and this will all be over in a week or so. "You with me?"

"Of course I am, it will be my pleasure to be rid of Vanessa so we can live the life of the rich and famous."

Little do they know Vanessa is up on Jarvis dirt she just don't know they are trying to kill her. Now, Vanessa really has to be on her toes with the display of anger Jarvis showed her earlier. Vanessa hear Jarvis as he is coming into the house. She is holding an ice pack to her bruised throat. Jarvis walks in and totally ignores Vanessa as though she is a stranger in her own home. Vanessa calmly walks upstairs with a look of anger that would kill a Calvary.

"Vanessa have you seen my pajamas?"

Vanessa just ignores Jarvis as though he didn't say a word.

"I asked you a question Vanessa do you hear me talking to you?"

Vanessa continues to ignore Jarvis and goes into the bathroom to shower.

"Well fuck it then, I guess you mad huh?"

Jarvis hollering to Vanessa in the shower, Vanessa continues to ignore him. Jarvis puts his pajamas on and lay in the bed like he a king. Vanessa walks out refreshed from her shower strolls over to her vanity table sit and starts to brush her hair when Jarvis gets up walks over to her and just stare at her.

"So you call yourself mad or something Vanessa?"

"Are you kidding me Jarvis, look at my neck I have bruises and you have the nerve to ask me something so stupid, really Jarvis."

"Who, the hell you think you talking to with that tone?"

"What has gotten into you J, why are you treating me this way?"

Jarvis just gives Vanessa a nasty look and go downstairs and sleep on the couch.

The next morning Jarvis is up early waiting for his phone call to meet with the hit man.

Vanessa is angry and hurt and only wants Jarvis to leave so she can do some planning of her own. She is not taking anymore of his bull crap. Vanessa knows for sure now either Jarvis has plans to get rid of her or he is thinking divorcing her to get money. Jarvis gets his call and where to meet Brad for their transaction. Jarvis walks pass Vanessa and leaves without so much as good morning or good bye.

"Good the bastard is gone but I better get going with my plans as well because he has something in store for me and I want to be ready." Vanessa waits for about twenty minutes to make sure Jarvis is gone. Vanessa gives her cousin Odell a call. Any other time Odell would not answer Vanessa out of fear but now for some reason he feel better because he knows he didn't do anything it was those stupid friends of his but nonetheless he still feel bad it happened to his cousin.

"What up Vanessa how is everything?"

"I guess its ok, Odell I need a big favor from you, can you help me? Its really important."

"Well I guess I can try what's up?"

“Where are you I need to see you it’s a long story and I am going to need your full attention.”

Vanessa and Odell continue to talk, Odell is feeling a little fearful that Vanessa knows what happened but won’t let on. However, as Vanessa continues he knows she still has no idea, maybe, it’s time Odell man up and tell Vanessa what really happened but, he don’t want the family or Vanessa to hate his guts.

“Ok Vanessa where and when do you want to meet?”

“Can you meet me today?”

"I guess since it's still early, it is going to take me about and hour to get there."

"Ok meet me downtown at the Junction, you know where that is?"

"Yea"

"Cool, I will see you in an hour, Odell."

"Yea"

"Thanks"

They hang up Vanessa gets lil J ready and drop him at the daycare and head out to meet Odell.

Vanessa arrives at the Junction before Odell, she get a table in the corner out the way because she don't know where Jarvis

is and don't want to run into him.

Vanessa is looking around when she spot Odell.

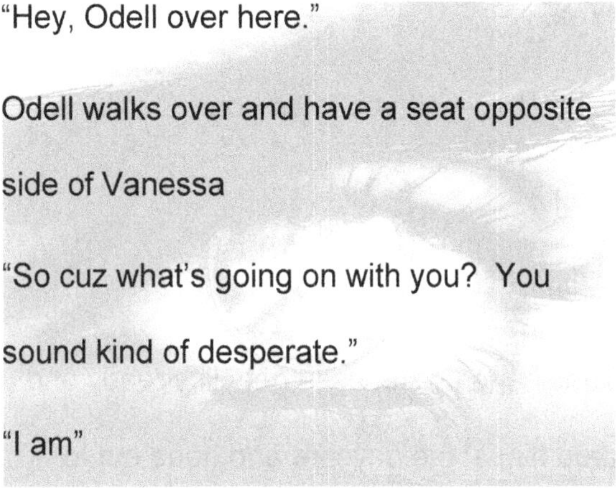

"Hey, Odell over here."

Odell walks over and have a seat opposite side of Vanessa

"So cuz what's going on with you? You sound kind of desperate."

"I am"

Vanessa begins to fidget with her cup of coffee.

"So tell me what's going on."

"Ok, I think Jarvis has been playing me all along, see something happened to me the night of our graduation party. I have no idea what happened I was drugged and somebody raped me, of course I got pregnant. Well Jarvis took on the responsibility of helping me through this but now its like he is a monster. He is hitting me."

"WHAT, hold on did you say hitting you?"

"Yes"

"So what you saying to me is the baby you have is not Jarvis and you have no idea who the baby father is?"

"Exactly, now, Odell you can't breathe a word of this to no one I am trusting you."

Now Odell feel even worse because he knows something happened but not sure now what happened when him and his home boys left. But now, he has a thought that maybe just maybe Jarvis had a hand in all this for some ulterior motive so he begins to question Vanessa.

"Listen, Vanessa I'm tripping on all this, have you ever thought it may have been Jarvis who raped you? Because why would he all of a sudden want to help you?"

"You know what Odell, that's a dam good question but I have a good idea."

"What"

"Money, see, I inherited some money and somehow he found out about it but once I realized it, it was too late we were already married."

"MARRIED, when did this all happen?"

"Christmas"

"That explains it cuz it sounds like he has some plans to get the money and I bet if you have the baby tested you will find out he is the father."

"Oh my God, Odell this all seems like a bad ass nightmare, I am afraid now, do you think he may be trying to kill me to get the money?"

"I could be wrong but it definitely sounds like he's up to something and I bet he is not working alone."

"This is too scary I feel like I am in a horror film."

"Listen to me Vanessa I want you to have the baby tested as soon as possible ok. Just continue to play it cool but watch your back and everything around you. When you get the baby tested, let me know and we will take it from there ok."

"Ok, Thanks Odell I knew I could count on you." Vanessa starts to cry.

"Don't cry man it's going to be alright now."

Vanessa gives Odell a hug and they leave, Vanessa head is spinning like a top she keeps trying to wake herself up from this terrible dream but only to realize it's reality..

In the meantime Jarvis is having a private meeting with the hit man.

"You got my money?"

"Yea, it's all there"

The hit man counts the money and looks at Jarvis sideways with an evil eye.

"When are you going to do it?"

"LISTEN PUNK I WILL DO IT IN MY TIME, DON'T QUESTION ME! I will call you when I set it up I need to check her out a few days. You just have my money or you will end up missing."

The hit man just get up and leave Jarvis sitting on the park bench. Jarvis calls Tranetta to let her know it has been set.

"You did it Jarvis, oh, I can see the money, did he say when."

"No, he said he has to tail her for a few days and he will call me when it's done."

"I hope he don't stiff you for the cash."

"I don't think so he's a professional."

"When can I see you Jarvis?"

"Right now, let's just play it cool for a few days."

"Jarvis, don't try nothing or you will go down man."

"Baby why would I try anything, we are in this together, don't you try anything. I love you Tranetta I would never do you wrong remember that baby."

"Yea, I'm sure that's the same lie you told Vanessa so just stick with the plan we can love one another later."

"Girl, you are too much I will call you in a few days."

Vanessa is at the pediatrician, she tells her the nurse that she needs a DNA for baby J. But, need the help of the nurse to get it done secretly. Vanessa offers the nurse a thousand dollars to help her.

"I don't know Vanessa what if I get caught?" as she whispers to Vanessa.

"You won't all you have to do is get the kit slip it to me and I will handle the rest."

"I can't risk my job."

"Ok, how about two thousand?"

"Vanessa, I got an idea, listen you can get the kit from the store and do it at home."

"They sell them in the store?"

"Sure, you can get it at any drug store."

"I feel so stupid, please forgive me I was just desperate."

"Forget about it I won't mention it, just be careful and let me know I just want everything to turn out good for you ok."

"Thank you so much, here take this hundred anyway . I won't say a word it's our secret."

Vanessa immediately goes to the nearest drug store and the nurse was right she purchased the kit and head off to get baby J. Back at the house Vanessa is so nervous she can hardly think, wondering what Jarvis next move is. Vanessa looks out the window and see a car she don't recognize. When the hit man sees her looking out the window he pulls off. Jarvis is pulling into the drive way and Vanessa runs upstairs to hide the kit hoping to swab him when he is sleeping but first she has to get him into a sound sleep when she remember she has some vicodin.

"Hey J you're home early how was your day?"

"It was ok" Jarvis answers Vanessa with a stale voice.

"I want to talk to you J" Vanessa trying to bait him in.

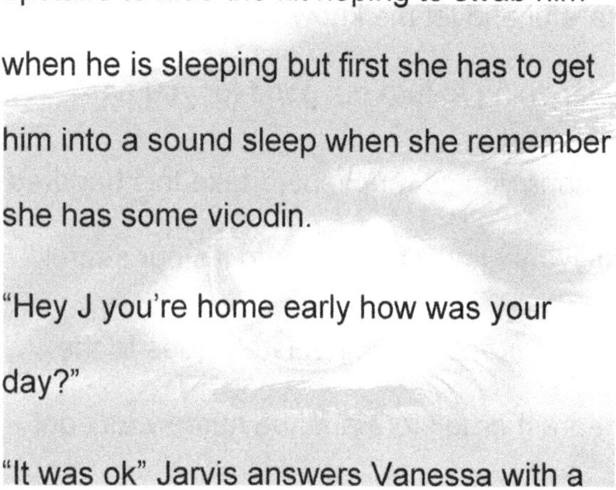

"I don't feel like it right now maybe in a few."

Vanessa backs off from Jarvis and goes to the kitchen to start dinner, hoping Jarvis will lighten up so she can get him where she want him. Jarvis comes into the kitchen and looks at Vanessa and starts to lighten up a bit with apologies so he can throw her suspicion off but, too late she is on to him.

"Vanessa, how about we start this day over?"

"I'd like that"

"I don't want you mad at me, sometime I can be such an ass hole please forgive me.

I got a great idea how about I cook dinner with you ok."

"Sounds like fun to me, how about I get us a cold glass of wine."

"Ok baby, you pour us some wine and I will get some music from upstairs, I will be right back."

Vanessa is clear for the plan, she quickly get the glasses of wine poured and put the Vicodin in Jarvis drink a nice big amount enough to knock him out all night. When Jarvis returns he puts the music on and toast Vanessa and takes his drink down quick.

After about thirty minutes Jarvis is dizzy and wants to lay down.

“What’s wrong honey?”

“I feel tired I think I will call it a night.” Jarvis unsuspecting of Vanessa.

“I will be up in a minute I need to make sure lil J is ok.”

Jarvis goes upstairs and is out before his head can hit the pillow. Vanessa quietly gets the test and just as she is about to swab his mouth Tranetta text him with a little good night note.

“Hey J I’m naked and wish you were here to give it to me good.”

Vanessa reads the text with her mouth open, when all of a sudden it hit her that Tranetta is probably working with Jarvis that's why she got all buddy with her again. Vanessa can't think about that now and decides to handle her later. She proceeds with her plan. Vanessa is thinking this is too easy "Look at this fool with his mouth wide open, thank you Mr. Nasty dog!" Then she swab herself and lil J. Vanessa is in control now with Jarvis passed out and the text from Tranetta is a God send because now she has information about them that they don't know about so this gets her out of the dark. Vanessa is smiling as she lays in bed finally able to get a good night's rest.

Thursday morning and Vanessa is up early and gone before Jarvis awakens. Vanessa is one up on Jarvis, however, she have no clue she is being followed by the hit man who Jarvis has hired to kill her, every turn Vanessa makes so does the killer. Vanessa arrives at the day care with lil J, speaks with the attendant for a few seconds and leave, as Vanessa is walking to her car she notice the same car has been following her so she decides to make sure instead of taking this as a coincidence. Vanessa leads the killer from one point to another.

"Oh, my God this guy is following me, this is not good, Jarvis is going to far now with a private investigator really."

Vanessa thinks the killer is just a private investigator but, never has Vanessa been so wrong, this is real and he is a ruthless, cold hearted killer. Vanessa goes to the mall with the killer close behind. Vanessa goes into one of the bigger department stores and goes into the bathroom so she can call Odell to tell him of her findings. After leaving Odell a message, Vanessa then take the swabs and directions for the results of the DNA test she took last night.

Vanessa finishes the test and wait the few minutes for the results. Lo and behold the DNA to Jarvis and Lil J is a perfect match, Vanessa can hardly believe her eyes. Vanessa feels as the the floor and ceiling is caving in on her with every little thing that has happened now is more clear than ever and the private investigator just maybe her killer. Vanessa gets herself together in the bathroom and as she is leaving Odell returns her call.

"Odell listen to me I want you to stay where you are I need to handle this and I do not want to get you involved because the stakes are higher now and it just may involve murder."

"I know you are kidding me right?"

"No Odell I wish I was this is not a joke."

"What makes you think murder may be involved in all this?"

"First of all there has been a guy following me for a few days now, I thought it was just some coincidence but , no this guy is definitely following me now, he can be either a P.I. or a hired killer, it does not matter either one my life is in danger I can feel it. Then, second, here's the real deal the DNA test to Jarvis and Lil J is a perfect match."

"What! I can't believe this dude, listen Vanessa get Lil J and get out of there. This guy has been playing you all along to get to your inheritance. I believe the guy following you may be a hit man."

"Here's another idea, I think Tranetta is working with him."

"Why you say that?"

"Last night when Jarvis was asleep Tranetta text him a sexy text and to me seems like they have been getting it on for a while, Tranetta all of a sudden wanted to be cool with me again, what an idiot I feel like a stupid ass fool."

"I can get to Tranetta if you want me too you know we were cool."

"No, I will take care of little Miss Tranetta, I do need you to come to meet me I have a plan to throw them off."

"Ok, how we going to do that with this guy following you?"

"Come to Lil J's daycare and come in as though you are picking up your kid and I will have some things for us, I already called Jena at the center she is going to play it off with us. Meet me there in about a hour ok."

"OK I will see you then, oh where the hell is the daycare."

Vanessa laughs because everything is planned and she forgot to tell him where the daycare is.

"My bad Odell come to texas ave. and Congress make a right on Congress and the daycare sit to the right it's a colorful kid friendly building you can't miss it."

"Cool, I am on my way."

They hang up from one another and Vanessa heads to the daycare with the killer in close tow. Vanessa goes into the daycare and chats with Jena for a minute. Odell comes in and Jena sends him to the bathroom where Vanessa is Jena has given Vanessa a wig. Odell and Vanessa switch clothes, Jena quickly puts some makeup on Odell and Vanessa slips in Odell's outfit. Jena gives Odell and Vanessa the final touches and the switch begins.

"Odell I want you to go to the movies and hang out there, while I go to take care of some things myself I will call you when I am done."

"Ok"

Vanessa and Odell head out one then the other Vanessa watches as Odell leaves with the killer in tow, Vanessa leaves and heads to a near by gun shop where she purchase a nine millimeter. Vanessa shows the man Odell's id as though she is him. This way the killer can't see that she has got some protection. Vanessa is in a totally different frame of mind now, as she looks at her purchase with revenge in her eyes and un-forgiveness in her heart. Vanessa calls Odell to let him know the coast is clear and to meet her back at the daycare show they can change again. They meet back at the daycare where the killer is now following

Vanessa once again with no clue to who Odell is. Vanessa leaves and goes home with Lil J to see if Jarvis is there. Vanessa arrives home

"Hello, Jarvis are you home?"

Vanessa gets no answer but Jarvis car is in the driveway. Vanessa takes sleeping Lil J upstairs and puts him to bed. Then, Vanessa goes back downstairs to the kitchen with the thought that someone must have come by and gave Jarvis a ride somewhere. Jarvis and Tranetta is so involved with their love making in the guest room that they didn't hear Vanessa come in until Lil J starts to cry this alarms Jarvis.

Jarvis Quickly looks out the window and sees Vanessa's car in the driveway. Quickly, tranetta gets out of bed dresses and hides in the closet, as Vanessa gets to the top of the stairs Jarvis appears as though he has been sleeping in the guest bedroom.

"Hey baby when did you get home?"

"Just a little while ago I called out to you. I thought you were gone with someone else when I didn't get a answer from you."

"Oh, I guess I didn't hear you I was in the other bedroom sleeping. I was feeling tired from working in the office. I thought you were gone to class, I decided to stay home today and get some paperwork done."

"Are you hungry I can make some lunch."

"Sure, I'm starving, here let me tend to J and you go do your thing girl."

"Ok I will call you when its ready."

Vanessa goes back down stairs not knowing Tranetta is hiding in the closet. Jarvis makes sure Vanessa is downstairs and goes back in to get Tranetta out the house.

"Man that was close, good thing you parked on the next street."

"Yea, we can't get caught now, you go divert her attention and I will slip out the side door."

"Good idea, listen, let's not play it close again. I will call you when she is done so we can start working on alibi's ok."

"Ok baby I will see you soon now go."

Jarvis goes downstairs to the kitchen and start lovingly talking to Vanessa with a little sweet horse play while Tranetta eases out the side door. The killer is watching Tranetta as she makes her get away. Vanessa is thinking in the back of her mind how dirty Jarvis is and how she has the jump on him. Vanessa is also thinking now that Jarvis had something to do with Sheka's murder and wonders if Tranetta helped him Vanessa continues to play Jarvis as though she does not suspect a thing.

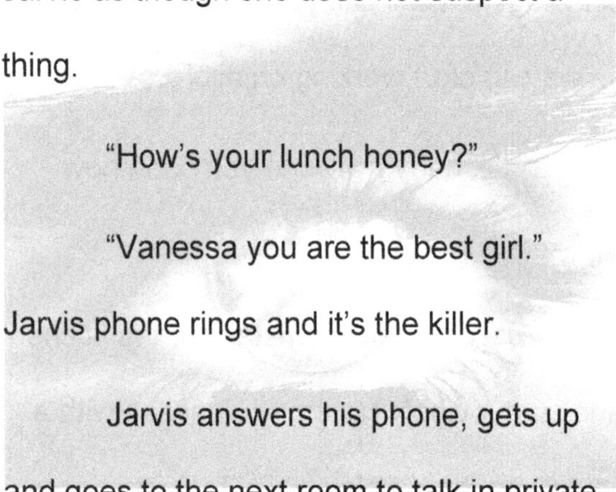

"How's your lunch honey?"

"Vanessa you are the best girl."

Jarvis phone rings and it's the killer.

Jarvis answers his phone, gets up and goes to the next room to talk in private.

"Hey lover boy I know what you're up. I saw your piece of ass leave. I been following her and now I am ready to make my move. I need you to be out of the house tomorrow so you need to come up with a plan for her to be there. I need everything to be quiet so I can come in and do my job got it?"

"Yea, but not the baby, you have to make this look like a home burglary so I will leave about six in the morning, I will leave the alarm off. Go to the side entrance and it will be open and when you finish, lock the door then break the glass." Jarvis is whispering to make sure Vanessa doesn't hear him.

"That works for me, don't come back until I call you I don't want you walking in messing up my plans. You just make sure when I call you be ready to meet me with my money then we will part ways." The killer hangs up and Jarvis goes back into the dining room, happy.

"So who was that on the phone honey?"

"That was Ken one of the investors for the café, I am excited everything is in order. However, I have to fly out to California early tomorrow to meet with the rest of the group so we can start building."

"That's great Jarvis, when will you be back?"

"I'm not sure, but, I will try to get it all done by the evening and I will probably take a late flight back if not the next day for sure but I will call you and let you know."

"OK, do you need me to help you pack?"

"No sweetie, I do need to run out and get some travel needs, so I will be back in just a few." Jarvis leaves but only to head to Tranetta's with the news. Jarvis enters Tranetta's place with a big smile, sweeps her off her feet and dances her around in his arms. Now, Jarvis is being followed by Odell. Odell wants to keep a close eye out for Tranetta and Jarvis to make sure that

Vanessa is ok. Odell is thinking this is the least I can do to make up for his indiscretion.

“Jarvis what’s going on why are you so happy?”

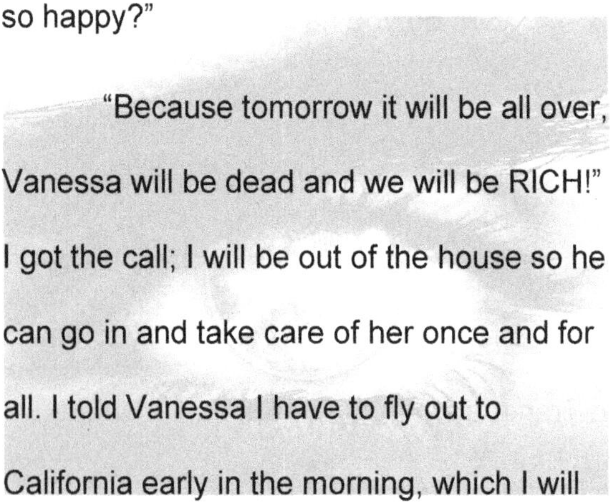

“Because tomorrow it will be all over, Vanessa will be dead and we will be RICH!” I got the call; I will be out of the house so he can go in and take care of her once and for all. I told Vanessa I have to fly out to California early in the morning, which I will do to have a great alibi and you stay here and go about your business as usual go to class that way if anything comes up you will have an alibi as well.”

"Oh Jarvis I am so happy this will soon be over." But, Tranetta is thinking of how to get rid of Jarvis as soon as she can to get the money because she has some plans of her own.

"I need to get to the store and pick up a few things I told Vanessa I needed so I will definitely call you when its done. Please, don't make a move until you hear from me."

Jarvis gives Tranetta a big kiss and leaves with Odell closely following him. Jarvis gets his things and head back to the house to pack.

"Hey Vanessa I'm back."

"Hey honey did you get everything you need?" When Jarvis left Vanessa did some snooping and found a withdrawal slip for fifty thousand dollars from an account she knew nothing about. Vanessa got an eerie feeling when she saw the withdrawal slip thinking to herself only reason a person would take out that kind of money would be to make a big purchase or have someone killed. The thought of Jarvis paying a hit man to kill her made her blood run cold.

"Yes, I got everything I need, so I do need to get packed now so I can go make us a good deal and we will be on easy street by the time we graduate from college."

"You are the man J." Vanessa is thinking to herself what a rat Jarvis is as she gives him a little grin.

Jarvis gives Vanessa a tap on her butt before running upstairs full of energy and excitement to pack so he can leave early.

Its five a.m. and Jarvis is getting ready to leave when Vanessa wakes up to see him off.

"So, Ms. Lady what are your plans for today?"

"I thought I would stay home and watch Lil J he had a little sniffle and a slight fever last night."

"Really, oh my little man I hate it when he is feeling bad."

"He will be fine he has his mommy to take care of him."

"I know and you are the best mommy in the world. But, if you need me don't hesitate to call and I will come right back, my son is more important than anything else." Jarvis grabs his bags and turns to Vanessa for a kiss. Since Vanessa is up he has to come up with a quick plan so she does not check the door or alarm.

"Vanessa why don't you lay back down and get some rest while the baby is sleeping I will make sure the doors are locked and the alarm is on."

"Have a safe trip baby and I am going to do just that so I can be ready for the baby when he wakes up thank you sweetheart and make sure you call me when you get to California to let me know you are safe. I don't want anything happening to you." Jarvis leaves and calls the hit man to tell him everything is clear. The killer lets Jarvis know he is near by and ready.

"Give it about thirty minutes before you go in because she was going back to bed and it usually takes her a few minutes to get back to sleep but other than that its all good."

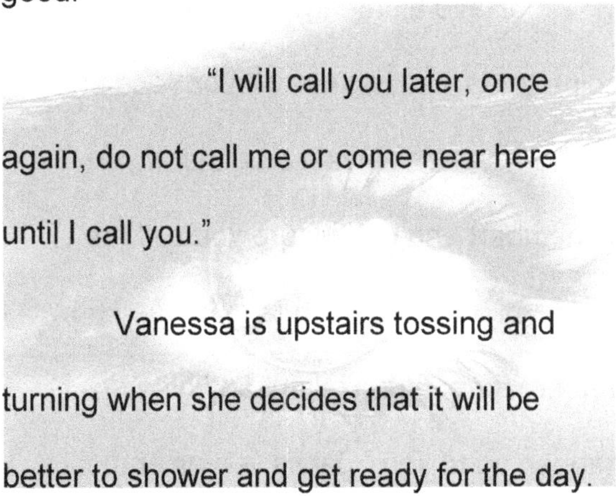

"I will call you later, once again, do not call me or come near here until I call you."

Vanessa is upstairs tossing and turning when she decides that it will be better to shower and get ready for the day. Vanessa is in the shower when the killer comes in and heads his way upstairs. The killer is dressed in all black with black gloves and a nine millimeter with a silencer.

He quietly creeps upstairs slowly opens the bedroom door and find that Vanessa is not in bed. He hears the shower turn off and goes into the closet to hide. Vanessa comes out of the shower; sit on the bed and start to dry off. The hitman is watching her every move. Vanessa's cell phone rings its Odell.

"Vanessa, I need you to listen to me carefully, get the baby and get out of the house, I saw Jarvis leave and someone is in your house."

"What, Odell what are you talking about?"

"I have been following Jarvis and I also notice there is someone following you Vanessa just get the baby and get out I am on my way I will explain to you more when I get there."

Vanessa now frantic at what Odell just told her nervously gets up and starts to walk toward the baby room when the hit man jumps out of the closet. Vanessa kicks him in the groin before he gets a shot off. Vanessa runs into the nursery and tries to get Lil J and as she bends over the hit man grabs her from behind choking her. Vanessa stomps his foot and elbows him in the stomach and run again, Vanessa runs downstairs and as she gets to the last step the hit man grabs her again and throws her to the floor and points his gun at her. Just as he is about to shout Odell bust in fires two shots into the hit man , startled that Odell has shot him he runs as fast as he can out the side door, Odell tries to catch him but he is running too fast.

"Vanessa are you alright?"

Vanessa is bruised and terrified just shakes her head for yes to let Odell know she is ok.

"Come on get up and let's call the police."

"Odell do you think Jarvis sent that guy?"

"Of course, he conveniently left so you could be killed, I have been following Jarvis and as I thought he went straight to Tranetta's."

"What should I do now? Jarvis is going to be looking for this guy to tell him I'm dead, Oh my God Odell I am so scared."

"Now that the puzzle has come together, just work with the police and get those bastards locked up. By the way what were the results to the test?"

"Lil j belongs to Jarvis. I am so stupid, he is the one who raped me and I have been living with this monster."

Vanessa has called the police, her and Odell wait for them to come. Once the police arrive they look the house over and question Vanessa with Odell by her side. Odell feels total relief knowing one of his friends did not father Vanessa baby. Jarvis has landed in California, all smiles as he walks through the airport thinking he will soon get a call confirming Vanessa is dead. In the meantime the hit man is wounded in the arm and left side but he is ok. He goes to one of his goon friends to get fixed up.

Once he is bandaged with a sling on his arm he calls Jarvis. Jarvis sees his call and rushes to receive his call.

"Hello"

"There was a problem."

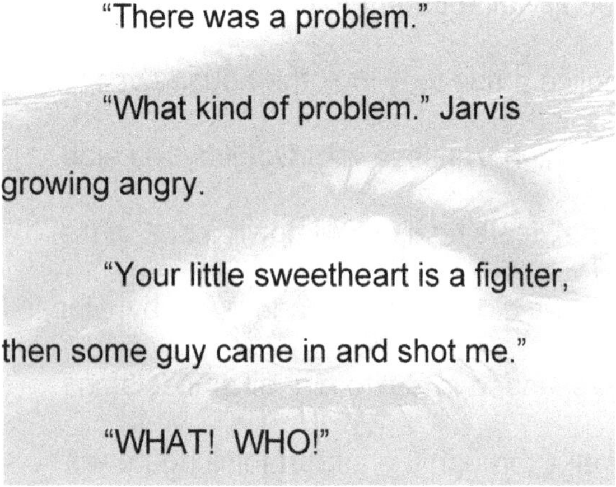

"What kind of problem." Jarvis growing angry.

"Your little sweetheart is a fighter, then some guy came in and shot me."

"WHAT! WHO!"

"I don't know, but I got out of there, I'm sure cops are all over the place by now."

"I cannot believe you messed this up."

"Listen you little wimp, I am professional, you the one can't plan."

Jarvis is nervous and don't know what to do.

"Did they see your face?"

"No I was well cover and got away before anything else happened."

"Ok, just sit tight and don't do anything else until I call you."

They hang up and Jarvis calls Tranetta to let her know what happened.

"Is it over Jarvis?"

"No, there was a problem, Vanessa seems to be stronger than we thought and besides he says some guy came in and shot him."

"What, who is this guy?"

"I have no idea, I need you to go over and see what's going on."

"I'm on it."

Tranetta hangs up from Jarvis and quickly dresses to go over to Vanessa's. The police has all the information they need and assure Vanessa they will patrol the neighborhood and look for the intruder. Odell comforts Vanessa.

"Vanessa I have to go and pick up some things but, I will be back make sure you lock the door and turn on the alarm. Make dam sure you don't give anything away to Jarvis or Tranetta just play along with them."

"Ok, Odell, I have never been so scared in my life."

"Just be cool I will be nearby, I am going to get some transmitters so I can hear every move Jarvis make when he get home just be cool I got you cuz and remember don't mention my name at all they don't need to know I am helping you."

Vanessa gives Odell A big hug and Odell leaves. Vanessa quickly locks herself in and turn on the alarm. The last officer is pulling away as Tranetta drives into the drive way the detectives are watching Tranetta as she walks to the door and rings the door bell.

"Vanessa what's going on I see police leaving and you seem to be shaken."

"Come in, I need to calm down, I had an intruder here this morning."

"What! Vanessa are you and the baby ok?"

"Yes we're good."

"Where's Jarvis?"

"He's in California"

"Have you called him yet?"

"No, I haven't had a chance I was talking to the police." Just as Vanessa says that Jarvis calls.

"Hey baby I made it safe, how is my lil man doing?" Vanessa plays him off.

"Jarvis baby there was an intruder in the house this morning." Tranetta listening closely.

"What! Baby are you and the baby ok, did he hurt you?"

"We are good he bruised me pretty bad but the baby is good. He slept through the whole ordeal."

"Did you call the police?"

"Yes they came and are now looking for the guy."

"How did you get him away from you?"

"Mr. Bill next door heard the loud commotion with me screaming and kicked in the door and shot him twice." Vanessa knew Bill and his family were leaving for a month this afternoon and Jarvis wouldn't be able to question him.

"I will be home right after the meeting on the next flight, make sure you stay safe. I wish you had a gun to protect yourself. We will work on getting you one ok baby." Vanessa is thinking to herself "you stupid ass I got one already, Vanessa has a little smirk on her face as she continues to play Jarvis.

"Get home soon honey, I am so scared."

"I will see you soon, love you."

"Love you too." They hang up; Vanessa has a bad taste in her mouth after having to tell Jarvis she loves him.

"Was that Jarvis?"

"Yea he's coming home on the next flight."

"Good, I won't have to worry so much with your husband home with you."

Odell is back at Vanessa's but see's Tranetta's car outside and calls Vanessa.

"I know Tranetta is in there, I need you to get her out so I can get these bugs in before Jarvis gets back." Vanessa plays it off like she is talking to her Mother. Her and Odell hang up and Vanessa is trying to get Tranetta out.

'That was my Mother she is worried about me. Listen, Tranetta I am wiped out and just want to get some rest can I call you later?"

"Are you sure you're going to be alright?"

"I will be fine, Bill is next door and I will have the alarm on."

"Ok well I will get out of your way, let me know if you need anything I will be home ok."

'Ok I will see you later."

Tranetta gives Vanessa a hug and leaves. Odell and the detectives watch as Tranetta leaves Odell waits about fifteen minutes just to make sure she is gone and goes in to hide the bugs for Vanessa.

"Thank you so much Odell I wouldn't know what to do without you."

"This should do it just make sure you keep him in the dark now so he don't get frantic and hurt you. I know its going to be hard but you can do it. Please don't tell uncle Terry we don't need him with a murder wrap."

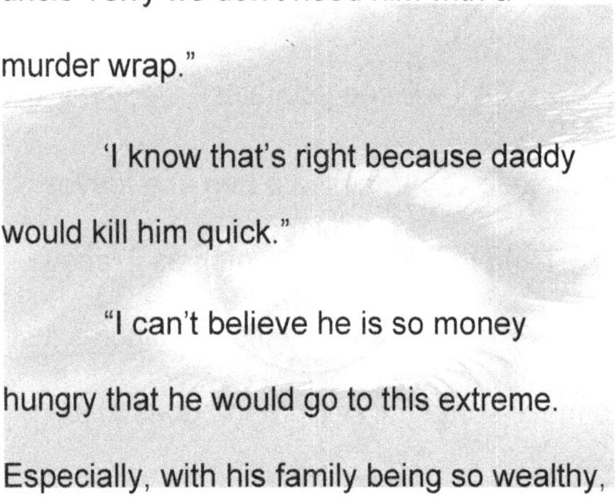

'I know that's right because daddy would kill him quick."

"I can't believe he is so money hungry that he would go to this extreme. Especially, with his family being so wealthy, what an ass hole."

"I'm just as confused as you are Odell. Jarvis is such a snake I can't wait to beat him at his own game. I just hope no one else gets hurt."

"Don't worry we just need to get him on tape so the police can arrest him. I need to go so I am going to leave you with my gun just in case that guy comes back."

Vanessa reaches around the back of her body and takes her nine millimeter out and shows it to Odell and his eyes get big.

"Oh snap cuz I didn't know you were strapped."

"I got it the other day when all the mess started to come together.'

"Well, I'm out. Oh yea what did Ms. Tranetta scandalous ass want?"

"Bitch playing like she is so concerned I should have popped her ass."

"Nope, don't worry she will get hers. I will be in contact soon stay safe."

Odell leaves but will be close by watching Jarvis. Tranetta is so mad that Vanessa is still alive. She goes home and waits for Jarvis to call her.

Jarvis is trying desperately to get another flight out but can't until later that night. Vanessa is feeling better knowing the detectives and Odell is there to help her get through this nightmare. The hit man is waiting to hear back from Jarvis as well. The evening sun is going down and the night seems to be exceptionally dark to Vanessa as she tries to put this horrifying day behind her. Vanessa is relaxed after a hot cup of peppermint tea and decides to check all the doors and alarm, she scoops lil j in her arms and head upstairs.

Tranetta is growing more and more angry by the moment that Vanessa is still alive she decides to wait until later to use her key sneak in and finish Vanessa herself. Its two thirty a.m. Tranetta dresses in all black goes into the neighborhood and parks three streets over. Carefully she scans the neighborhood and notices a strange car with two men asleep. Tranetta laughs at how stupid they look. She continues to the house un noticed even by Odell who is outside watching as well. Tranetta, carefully unlocks the door and quickly goes in tips to the alarm and punch in the code. Vanessa is sound asleep with baby J right beside her.

Tranetta, feels her way in the dark quietly not to wake Vanessa, her plan is to go in and stab her to death and leave. Vanessa feels the need to get a drink and gets up flips her lamp on, Tranetta hears her and quickly but quietly goes back downstairs and hides in the darkness of the living room. Vanessa comes downstairs goes into the kitchen get her an apple juice and as she is heading back upstairs she notice a silhouette sitting in the recliner staring at her. Vanessa switch on the lamp by the stairs and Tranetta is sitting there in all black.

"Tranetta is that you. What are you doing sitting in my house in the dark with all black on?"

Tranetta gets up slowly and starts to walk toward Vanessa holding the knife when Jarvis walks in.

"Tranetta what the hell you doing here?"

"You dumb ass somebody needs to finish this bitch off and what better person than me I should have done it myself in the beginning but no Mr. Jarvis wants' to get a stupid fucken hit man that can't spell his OWN FREAKING NAME!"

"Tranetta, go home and leave this to me, you are going to mess it all up."

Vanessa looks on in fear. Trying to see how she can get upstairs and get her gun as they are arguing back and forth Vanessa makes a move towards upstairs when Tranetta runs over and punches her in the face knocking her to the floor and get on top of her and starts screaming at Vanessa. Jarvis goes over to Tranetta and grabs her and tells her that she is screwing up. Tranetta goes into her bag and gets some tape and bound Vanessa hands, feet & mouth and sits her in a chair.

"Now what Tranetta? She knows now, are you crazy?"

"Its simple let me kill her no one knows I'm here, I can kill her, leave and you can say you found her this way. It's the perfect plan."

Vanessa is horrified, struggling to get away Odell hears this and carefully sneaks around the back to see how he can get in without them seeing him. Vanessa continues to struggling and makes sounds. Jarvis walks over to Vanessa and slaps her. Tranetta begins to laugh with a loud wicked laugh. Tranetta walks over to Vanessa and snatches the tape from her mouth.

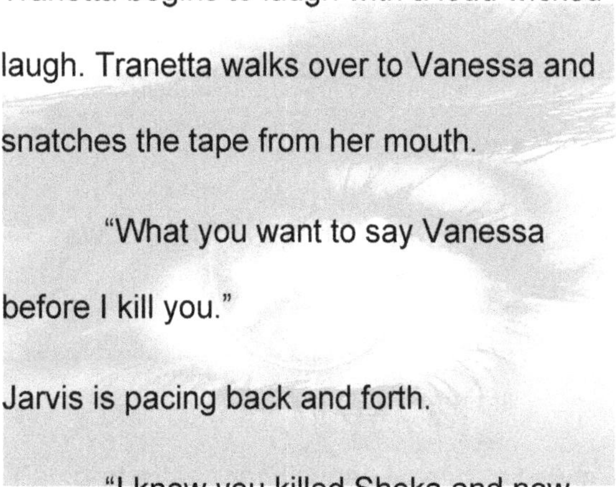

"What you want to say Vanessa before I kill you."

Jarvis is pacing back and forth.

"I know you killed Sheka and now you want to kill me I figured it out. You think you gonna get paid, ha, Jarvis will kill you too."

"You don't worry about me and Jarvis. Besides it took your little dumb ass long enough yea I killed Sheka and it felt good. Jarvis and I are about to be very rich and you about to be very dead."

"Well, before you kill me you should know Jarvis is a rapist who raped me and got me pregnant, yea J I had a DNA done and you're the father. You stole my innocence and played as though you cared so much, well I been on to you both, so go ahead kill me it will all be for nothing because I changed my will, bank accounts and insurance so you two fools will GET

NOTHING!!! Vanessa then does her own wicked laugh.

Before they could make their next move Odell comes up behind Jarvis and puts his gun to his head.

"Well, well, well look what I got two birds with one stone Jarvis and his piece of shit girlfriend."

Tranetta breaks in a rage and runs for Odell with her knife up Odell stands back and shoots Tranetta in the arm knocking the knife out of her hand. Tranetta falls to the floor and screams in pain. The detectives hear the shot and rushes to Vanessa's. Jarvis moves in on Odell and knocks the gun out of his hand and they begin a fight tossing one another around the room. As they are fighting the detectives are getting closer to the house, Tranetta struggles up and gets the gun she's close enough to Vanessa who takes both bound feet and kick Tranetta as hard as she can knocking Tranetta into the fireplace and a big vase falls and knocks her out. Jarvis and Odell continue to man handle each other.

Jarvis hits Odell and knocks him over the sofa and runs grabs the gun, Odell gets up and Jarvis is pointing the gun at Odell when detective Bates fires a shot hitting Jarvis in the leg. Jarvis drops the gun and the detectives move in with their weapons on Jarvis and Tranetta. Odell runs over to Vanessa and release her from bondage and gives her a big hug. Police are everywhere, Tranetta and Jarvis is arrested for conspiracy to commit murder.

ONE MONTH LATER

Jarvis and Tranetta is being sentenced along with the hit man whose name is Brad Coleman. The investigation led them to the hit man from Jarvis phone records. The tape Odell planted had the culprits on it which also solved the murder of Sheka. Jarvis and Tranetta was sentenced to life without parole for Sheka's murder and the hit man got ten to fifteen for attempted murder on Vanessa. When they are sentenced Vanessa and her family gave a loud clap and Jarvis parents broke down in tears.

SIX YEARS LATER

Vanessa is now a Nurse Practitioner with a thriving Pediatrician office. Lil Jarvis is happy and healthy. Vanessa goes to the day care picks up Jarvis and goes to the beach and watch the sun go down with Little Jarvis along side her playing in the sand.

Conclusion

The characters depicted in this story relates to no specific individual or individuals it is all fictional and for reading purposes only. The author Betty Knight Taylor is creative in story telling to heighten the reader imagination. Betty is also a playwright with a hit stage play from her book "Drama, Lies & Deceit." She is also the author of "Hallelujah I am Woman" which is a motivational for women to help them stay focused as they proceed to there desired destinations. She has two other books,

Stolen Treasures & Full grown man, full grown woman. You can purchase copies through www.lulu.com/author 2008 or go to her website

www.taylormadeproductions1.webs.com

Mrs. Taylor is also a motivational speaker and upcoming film maker she is in the process of writing a movie script.

Mrs. Taylor is also a proud Mother, grandmother & wife.

Thank you all for your support for purchasing this book I hope it gave you as much pleasure reading it as it did in my writing it. Look for more of my titles to come and hopefully with blessings

and prayers you will see my creations on the big screen.

Bessings & Love,

Betty Knight Taylor.

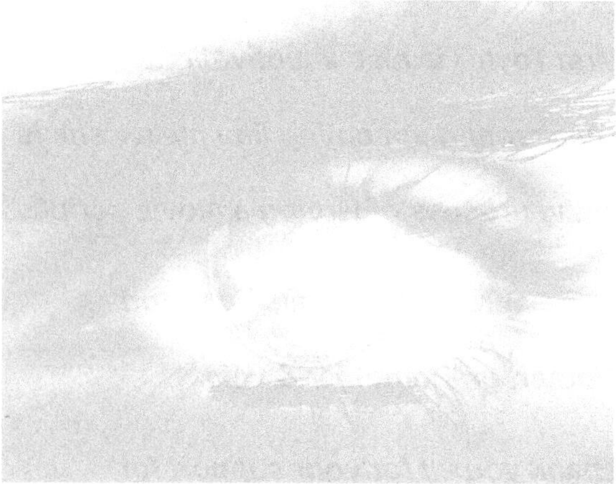